French Dressing

Roy Plomley

Weidenfeld and Nicolson
London

Published in Great Britain by
Weidenfeld and Nicolson
11 St John's Hill, London SW11

ISBN 0 297 77514 6

Printed in Great Britain by
Willmer Brothers Limited, Rock Ferry, Merseyside

F06986

To Marie

Contents

1913

1913

Monday, 8 September

The sky was clear and blue, the sun was gleaming on the white paintwork of the hotels, and striking golden shafts from the gilded dome of the casino : a lizard was scuttling among the roots of a tamarisk tree. Already it was warm, and Commissaire Emile Bonpain removed his straw hat and carried it in his hand. His pace was a little quicker than usual, because there was a heavy day's work ahead. He was a tall, powerfully-built man with a lugubrious and distrustful expression : his small moustache was of the type to be made famous within a few years by a young Englishman named Chaplin.

From the Avenue Victor-Hugo, he turned left into the Rue Thiers, which led to the sea front. The palm-shaded gardens on his left were being watered by a blue-smocked man wielding a heavy hose. The man paused to mop his forehead and, to free his hands, clutched the spouting nozzle between his thighs, producing a cheerfully obscene effect.

A gleaming Dion-Bouton tourer, driven by a chauffeur wearing goggles and a hot serge uniform, whirred by sending up a cloud of white dust. In the back of the open car sat a middle-aged couple swathed in cotton dustcoats; on the luggage grid was strapped a pile of expensive leather suitcases. Thanks to judicious advertising in better-class periodicals, the holiday season was proving most successful.

On the sea-front corner towered the western flank of the Grand Hotel of the Baths and of Serbia. Before the porticoed entrance in the Rue Thiers the automobile stopped, and two porters in striped waistcoats trotted down the hotel steps to lift the suitcases from the grid, while the chauffeur assisted the middle-aged couple to alight. They stood on the pavement, beating the dust from their coats. The man

1

removed his goggles, revealing two swarthy circles on his white-dusted face.

Commissaire Bonpain followed the porters up the steps and looked through the glass doors. He saw Inspector Léonard Hanoteau standing unobtrusively by the reception desk, his dark hooded eyes ceaselessly surveying everything that was going on in the vast lobby. He was a good man, Hanoteau.

The commissaire descended the steps and looked to right and left. Where was Inspector Gibeau, who should be patrolling the exterior of the building? Bonpain walked down to the corner and looked along the frontage which faced the sea, and then he came back past the entrance. He saw Gibeau's plump form waddle out of an alley which led to the staff entrance; he was stuffing a croissant into his mouth. When he saw Bonpain, he straightened up, tried to swallow it at a gulp, failed, and removed some of it from his mouth with his fingers, slipping it into a pocket with what he hoped was a surreptitious gesture.

Bonpain looked at him sternly. 'Anything to report, Gibeau?' he asked.

'Nothing, *Monsieur le Commissaire*,' he mumbled. Then the rest of the food went down, and the remainder of his speech was clearer. 'I've only just come on duty.'

Bonpain regarded his subordinate from face to feet, taking in the three chins, the croissant crumbs down the waistcoat, the fat stomach, the baggy trousers and the scuffed black boots. Without doubt, Gibeau was a disaster of a detective.

'Keep alert,' said Bonpain.

'Yes, *Monsieur le Commissaire*.'

'It is during the changeover of duties that carelessness occurs and opportunities are taken. Watch it.' Bonpain turned and walked briskly away.

The commissariat was housed in a wing of the municipal casino, and Bonpain's first-floor office looked across the promenade to the sea. The beach was deserted except for the middle-aged English novelist whose sales were reputed to equal those of Pierre Louÿs and Pierre Loti and the great Elinor Glyn. Every morning, attired in a bottle-green bathing costume, the lonely bald-headed man ran four kilometres along the sand.

Bonpain hung his hat on the bentwood stand and turned to face

Inspector Lautier, who had followed him into the room. Lautier was young and keen and bespectacled.

'Well?' asked Bonpain, sitting down at his cluttered desk.

Lautier consulted a notebook. 'Dinner was sent up to the suite at nine o'clock last night; the dishes were removed at eleven-fifteen, at which time the two gentlemen were sitting at a window, smoking cigars. Neither gentleman left the hotel. The lights in the main bedroom were put out at about midnight, and those in the subsidiary bedroom a few minutes later. This morning's report is not yet in.'

'I looked in at the hotel on my way here. I disturbed Gibeau at his breakfast.'

Lautier grinned.

'Gibeau is nothing to grin about; he's a weak link in the chain. Other matters?'

Lautier looked down again at his notebook. 'Two German yachtsmen were drunk and abusive outside the Café des Colonnes, and were put in the cells to cool down. They were released at daylight. I presume they will not be charged.'

'Certainly not; we want them to get drunk again tonight. The more money they leave in the town the better. Next?'

'An American called to complain that he had been overcharged at Madame Zizi's.'

'Which girl did he have?'

'He had two – Fifi and the big redhead.'

'What did you tell him?'

'That it was a matter for the *Syndicat d'Initiative* rather than the commissariat. I reminded him that this is a very high-class resort and that the prices must reflect the fact.'

'That was the right answer. If all the citizens work together, this town can put Deauville out of business.' Bonpain thought of the plot of land he had recently acquired on the outskirts of the town: already it had increased in value.

For the next two or three hours, matters were routine. From the Grand Hotel of the Baths and of Serbia came a report that the parties under surveillance had breakfasted in their rooms.

At eleven o'clock, the mayoral barouche came to a stop outside and the mayor himself, Edouard Tinville-Lacombe, ironmonger in the Place Masséna, was shown into the commissaire's office. His face was large and smooth and plump and white, and his dewlaps shook as he sat down.

'I hear we have a most distinguished visitor, *Monsieur le Commissaire.*'

'You didn't get that information from official sources, *Monsieur le Maire.*'

'No, *Monsieur le Commissaire.*'

The mayor offered no elaboration, and Bonpain sighed. 'What can I do for you?'

'As first citizen, I feel it my pleasurable duty to call upon him – with my wife, of course – to welcome him to our town, and to offer to do all in my power to make his brief stay here a happy one.'

'So you even know how long he's to stay.'

'A week, is it not?'

'Our royal guest is here strictly incognito. He is accompanied only by a personal friend . . .'

'The Englishman, Colonel Withers.'

'As you say. My task is to provide unobtrusive protection and make sure that their privacy is respected.'

'I gather that his well-being is not left entirely in your care; there is a man sent from Paris to keep an eye on him.'

'You know everything, *Monsieur le Maire.*'

'I'm told it's Monsieur Grunwald, who was on duty when the Crown Prince Helmut was here last year.'

'I congratulate you on the accuracy of your sources.'

'Now, I am mayor of this town . . .'

'Nobody is disputing the fact, but my instructions are to keep at bay even such notable citizens as yourself.'

'My wife happens to be related to the Bluchners, who are cousins by marriage of the Sieghoffs, whose illegitimate son was, for a while, secretary to His Majesty's father.'

'Even so, *Monsieur le Maire* . . .'

'My wife will be very displeased.'

'I'm sorry.'

The mayor rose to his feet. 'I shall remember this, Bonpain.'

Bonpain hastily surveyed in his mind the ill deeds that the mayor was likely to be able to serve him, decided that they were negligible and contented himself with a bow. The mayor swept out, and the rest of the morning was uneventful.

Bonpain was just about to go to lunch when the major event of the day, the week, the month, the year and his entire career, mani-

4

fested itself. Lautier burst into the room, his pale face shining with excitement.

'*Monsieur le Commissaire* . . .'

'There can be nothing that can't wait until after luncheon, Lautier.'

'*Monsieur le Commissaire*, it's – murder !'

Bonpain started. Since he had taken office in the town, some six years before, there had been assault, battery, burglary, rape, barratry, arson, abortion, larceny, fraud, simony and gross indecency but this was the first and only time that the big number had come up.

'Where?' he asked. 'Who?'

'At the bathing station. A woman.'

'A woman has been murdered?'

'A woman has murdered, *Monsieur le Commissaire*.'

'Is she in custody?'

'Verdi has her.'

'Let them come in.'

Inspector Verdi was a small, dark, fast-blinking man of Italian origin, and his captive, who was handcuffed to him, was a striking, fair and immensely attractive woman of about thirty. She wore a fashionably-cut silk dress in pale oatmeal, which moulded her large breasts and slim haunches: of ankle length, it was slit on each side to above the knee. On her head, a stockinette cap was set at a provocative angle. She seemed perfectly at home, looked round for a chair, selected the one facing Bonpain's desk and sat down in it, dragging Verdi half a pace towards her in doing so.

Bonpain summed her up, decided that the three males in the room could together overpower her if necessary, and signed to Verdi to unlock the handcuffs. There was a delay, as Verdi had put the key in the trousers pocket next to the lady and, as the chain was very short, her hand had almost to go into the pocket with his.

The commissaire liked to adopt a frightening attitude to prisoners who were brought before him, but in the case of this delectable female he found it impossible to do so; in fact, he found himself bowing slightly and speaking in a modulated voice as he said: 'Your papers.'

'At the hotel, monsieur,' replied the lady, softly and modestly.

'Which hotel?'

'The Hotel of the Loire and of the Golden Chariot.'

It was a good hotel, second only to the Grand Hotel of the Baths and of Serbia.

'Tell me,' said Bonpain to Verdi.

Verdi drew himself up to his full, if inconsiderable, height. 'I was in my office on the floor above, *Monsieur le Commissaire*. I happened to glance out of the window, and I noticed a disturbance at the bathing establishment.'

'What sort of disturbance?'

'There were people running to and fro, and Madame Berthier, the proprietress, was waving her arms in the air and showing every sign of distress.'

'Was there no sign of *Sergent de Ville* Maupas, who should have been patrolling this section of the promenade?'

'No, *Monsieur le Commissaire*. He was undoubtedly occupied elsewhere.' Everyone knew of the young *sergent de ville's* obsessive interest in the young woman who kept the beach toys shop opposite the Hotel of the Lighthouse and of the Three Crowns.

'Continue.'

'I went downstairs and crossed the promenade. Madame Berthier grabbed me by the arm and pointed to a dead man, saying that he'd been murdered.'

'Where was the deceased lying?'

'On the duckboards between the two rows of changing cabins, just a few paces from Madame Berthier's pay booth.'

'Has he been identified?'

'Not yet.'

'Had he the appearance of a person of quality?'

'Oh yes, *Monsieur le Commissaire*. His outer clothing is of the highest order, and his linen is of silk.'

Bonpain ignored the solecism. 'And in his pockets?'

'Nothing at all, except a handkerchief – again of silk – a gold watch and a considerable sum of money.'

'How considerable?'

'Three hundred and forty francs, *Monsieur le Commissaire*.'

Obviously, thought Bonpain, this was a case to be treated with the utmost seriousness. Aloud, he asked: 'How had he been murdered?'

'He had been stabbed, *Monsieur le Commissaire*.'

'Is Madame Berthier here?'

Inspector Lautier answered. 'She's waiting outside, *Monsieur le Commissaire.*'

'Bring her in. I prefer a testimony in the first person.'

Lautier went out, and returned with a large, tearful and elderly lady, who identified herself as Madame Berthier, Hortense, wife of Monsieur Berthier, Alphonse, turncock in the employ of the local waterworks. She was shaking her head from side to side and breathing stertorously.

'A chair,' commanded Bonpain, gallantly.

Verdi scuttled to fetch one, but his effort was wasted; in her distraught state, Madame Berthier preferred to stand, in which position she found it easier to take in the two-litre breaths with which she was oxygenizing her frame.

'Now, Madame,' said Bonpain, 'if justice is to be done, you must be explicit – and at once.'

Madame Berthier nodded. Lautier seated himself at a side table and poised a pen, ready to take notes.

'With this morning's fine weather,' said the witness, 'most of my cabins were occupied, either by the bathers themselves, or by the clothes of bathers who were in the water. Then, from number nine, came the gentleman.'

'Which gentleman?'

'The gentleman who was murdered,' interjected Verdi.

'I prefer to hear Madame Berthier's testimony,' said Bonpain.

'I'm sorry, *Monsieur le Commissaire.*'

'Which gentleman?' repeated Bonpain.

'A middle-aged gentleman with a round face and a small, black moustache, wearing a straw hat and a white tussore suit, who had arrived some minutes before.'

'This is the gentleman who is now dead?'

'Yes.'

'But obviously he wasn't dead when he came out of the cabin.'

'He was far from well.'

'You could immediately gather that?'

'His two hands were clutched to his face, and blood was running between his fingers.'

'He had been stabbed in the face?'

'To the side of the eye, *Monsieur le Commissaire.*'

'Did he say anything?'

'He called "Help" several times, then he fell to the ground.'

7

'To the duckboards,' corrected Verdi.

'You then discovered him to be dead ' asked Bonpain, ignoring the interruption.

'I suspected it,' said Madame Berthier.

'From whom did you seek corroboration?'

'Monsieur Peyronnet, the lifeguard.'

'Where is Monsieur Peyronnet, the lifeguard?' Bonpain asked Verdi.

'Guarding lives, *Monsieur le Commissaire*. I didn't feel myself justified in taking him away from his duties. If, during his absence, a bather should find himself in difficulties . . .'

'Yes, yes,' said Bonpain irritably. Murder it might be, but it was also a quarter of an hour after lunchtime. He turned back to Madame Berthier. 'Did you send for a doctor?'

'Monsieur Peyronnet did. The young Godefroi boy was nearby, building a sandcastle, and he was despatched to fetch Doctor Herriot.'

'In the meantime, there was the question of who had committed the murder.'

'Obviously. That had not escaped the attention of Monsieur Peyronnet and myself, *Monsieur le Commissaire*. The murdered gentleman had been alone in his cabin . . .'

'You are sure of that?'

'I run a respectable establishment.' Madame Berthier threw out her immense chest and bridled.

'If the gentleman was alone in the cabin, then who can have killed him?'

'If I may interject, *Monsieur le Commissaire*,' Verdi half raised a hand like an eager schoolboy. '*Monsieur le Commissaire* is perhaps forgetting that I was by now on the scene.'

'You have a theory, Verdi?'

'A theory which I hope *Monsieur le Commissaire* will agree provides a satisfactory explanation.'

'Proceed.'

'A cursory examination revealed that the wound, while deep enough to penetrate the brain and cause almost instant death, was inflicted by a very thin but very sharp weapon.'

'And where does that lead us?'

'To the adjoining cabin. In the dividing matchboarding is a hole, some fifty millimetres in diameter.'

'You are suggesting then . . . ?'

8

'Exactly, *Monsieur le Commissaire*. The wound was undoubtedly inflicted from the adjoining cabin.'

'By the side of the eye?'

'By the side of the eye.'

'Which leads us to assume ...'

'That the deceased gentleman had his eye to the hole.'

The commissaire turned severely to Madame Berthier. 'Is the facility for clandestine observation one of those provided at your establishment?'

'I swear before God, *Monsieur le Commissaire* ...'

'Nevertheless, it appears to happen.'

Lautier lifted his eyes from his notebook. 'As a regular patron of Madame Berthier's well-run establishment, it has been my observation that the sexes are normally separated, her female clients being directed into the row of cabins on the seaward or left-hand side, while her male clients are directed into those on the landward or right-hand side.'

'That is invariably my practice,' said Madame Berthier, emphatically.

'Not invariably,' said Verdi, with a triumphant air. 'In the adjoining cabin to the deceased gentleman was the lady here.' He indicated the lady to whom he had recently been handcuffed, and who had been taking only a detached interest in the proceedings.

'Ah!' said Bonpain.

Madame Berthier protested. 'I have already explained that it was a busy time, and I do not have eyes in the back of my head.'

'Some of your clients hardly have eyes at all,' said Verdi.

Bonpain silenced him with a glare. He turned again to Madame Berthier. 'Were the two adjoining cabins in question on the seaward, or left-hand side, or on the landward, or right-hand side?'

'On the left.'

'On the side to which female clients are directed?'

'Yes.'

'So the person who was out of place was the deceased?'

'Yes. He must have climbed over the fence.'

'Fence?' queried Bonpain.

Verdi leapt in to explain. 'There is a low trellis fence running down the middle of the establishment. It's a mere metre in height: a young man could vault it, an older man could clamber over it with ease.'

9

Bonpain turned to the blonde lady sitting in front of him. 'Until such time as we have obtained your papers from your hotel, will you be kind enough to tell us who you are?'

The lady lifted her large grey eyes to the commissaire and introduced herself. 'Masson, Ernestine.'

'Madame or Mademoiselle?'

'Madame.'

'Permanent address?'

'197, Avenue du Bois-de-Boulogne, Paris.'

'Do you plead Guilty or Not Guilty?'

'Of what?'

'Murder.'

'Not Guilty.'

'When the inspector asked you to leave the cabin you had been occupying, did you see the body of your late neighbour lying on the duckboards?'

'I saw a body lying on the duckboards.'

'Had you seen the man before?'

'Never.'

'You had been bathing?'

'I had.'

'I suggest that it was because of an understandable rage at finding yourself clandestinely observed by a strange man while performing various intimate and personal acts essential to a lady while dressing herself, that you decided to revenge yourself by striking him through the observation hole with some long, thin, sharp object, such as a hatpin.'

'If the man was observing me, how was I to know it?'

'Perhaps some involuntary ejaculation . . .'

All three listeners raised their heads sharply. Bonpain repeated the sentence, completing it. 'Perhaps some involuntary ejaculation may have been uttered by the man – or some sound, such as unusually heavy breathing.'

In a voice much too sweet for such shameless words, Madame Masson said: 'I'm not the kind of woman to be upset by the fact that an unknown man has seen me in my drawers.'

Madame Berthier pursed her lips in horror and disbelief, Verdi's chin dropped, Lautier made a blot: only the commissaire gave no outward sign of shock.

Madame Masson continued: 'The idea that I should stab someone in such circumstances is complete nonsense.'

'Nevertheless, Madame, there seems evidence ...'

'Evidence? What evidence? Where is the murder weapon? You say the deed could have been done with a hatpin: I wore no hat when I left the hotel, merely this cap, and therefore carried no hatpin.'

'Has the lady's handbag been searched?' asked Bonpain.

'It has, Monsieur le Commissaire.'

'No sharp implement?'

'Alas, no,' said Verdi, revealing his disappointment that this was no cut-and-dried case.

'Has the cabin been searched?'

'It has, Monsieur le Commissaire.'

'No chisel?' asked Madame Masson, sarcastically. 'No gimlet? Not even a knitting needle?'

'Further enquiries must be made,' said Bonpain. 'Keep this lady in custody, and we shall take the matter further at –' he consulted the large silver watch from his waistcoat pocket, '– at two thirty.' Heaven only knew what had happened to his luncheon during this unfortunate delay. If his Parisian wife had prepared one of his favourite *escalopes de veau à la mode de Barbès*, it would be quite dried up. He took his hat from the stand, and hurried from the room.

At midday, when the majority of bathers returned to their hotels for a light five-course luncheon, Madame Berthier's establishment closed for two hours. Normally, the proprietress padded off to the small house behind the *mairie* to prepare a meal for her turncock spouse, pausing at the butcher's on the way. Monsieur Peyronnet, the tall, handsome, patent-leather-haired lifeguard, after whom so many female holidaymakers sighed each season, moved next door to the little beach restaurant called Le Florida where, having donned a waiter's dress suit, he served luncheons until twenty minutes to two, at which time, the rush of customers having subsided, he sat in the kitchen and ate his own meal. It made for a long, hard day, but it was a short season and one had to make one's hay while the sun shone.

Today, he was the centre of attraction. Most of the lunchers had heard of the morning's tragedy, even if they had not been on hand to savour the exciting moments of the arrest of Madame Masson and the removal in a hand ambulance of the unknown corpse. Monsieur Peyronnet – Jules to his friends and fellow workers – was interrogated at length while he served the *salade niçoise*, the *carrelet grillé*, the *côte d'agneau* with runner beans, the local soft yellow cheese known as *chameaucrotte*, with fresh fruit to follow, and opened bottles of a reasonable wine from the vineyard of the proprietor's cousin at Buzet-sur-Baise. Peyronnet was a methodical man, who added up his *pourboires* every day and entered the total in a little red book, and he was happy to discover that the take was two hundred and fifty-six percent above the average for the time of year.

It was the erring *Sergent de Ville* Maupas, fresh from renewed dalliance with his lady at the beach toys shop, who delivered the convocation requiring him to attend at the commissariat at half past two.

'And if you're not there on the dot, my old Jules, the Minister of the Interior himself will be here after your balls,' said Maupas.

'And is the Minister of the Interior going to patrol the beach during my absence and see that no stupid swimmers get out of their depth, and sluice out the cabins after small children have done their *pipi* on the floor, and see that no immoral acts take place between bathers inflamed by the sight of the bare flesh of the opposite sex?'

'Even when you're here, my old Jules, it seems that immoral acts take place – if murder can be described as one.'

'I can't be held responsible for the acts of solitary persons in cabins.'

'You could plug the holes in the partitions.'

'And there'd be new ones the next day; it's the natural curiosity of the young.'

'Madame Berthier will be at the commissariat too, so you'll just have to close the place for the afternoon.'

Peyronnet tapped the side of his nose thoughtfully. 'That would present problems. We have many valuable objects in the establishment, such as the sand rake, and the bunting, and the deckchairs, and the towels for hiring out, and the frame for the weather chart, and the clocks showing the times of high tides, let alone a thousand other things which I shouldn't be able to store away securely by half past two. All these could easily be purloined if left unattended.'

'I'm a custodian of the law, Jules; I'll be leaning on the railings on the promenade, and if there's any irregularity it will be dealt with. Tell me about the blonde lady.'

'A whizzer, old chap. The best female swimmer I've ever seen on this beach, with a graceful walk, and a slim waist, and golden hair, and a pair of tits that could poke your eyes out.'

'I doubt if that's the method she used in the case of this morning's victim,' said Maupas.

'The metaphor slipped out thoughtlessly,' said Peyronnet. 'When will we know who the victim is?'

'My colleagues are checking the hotels now. The fact that no bathing costume or towel was found in his cabin seems to show that he had no intention of bathing.'

'Evidently.'

'In a respectable and properly-run establishment, such a thing would be observed and commented upon, and such a person refused admission.'

'His one franc fifty is as good as anyone else's,' said Peyronnet. 'It's not unknown for a passer-by to take a cabin for some personal matter quite unconnected with bathing, such as adjusting a truss.'

'That could be done in a public convenience for only ten centimes.'

'In a resort such as this, there are those to whom all coins with holes in them mean nothing.'

'That's a sign of real riches,' said Maupas, sighing.

In the damp gloom of the municipal Opera House, the dress rehearsal of *Lakmé* was about to begin.

The Opera House, a vast echoing place, had been built in the days of the first Napoleon as a sign of confidence in an Empire that would last forever, and how it had managed to get so dirty in only a hundred years was a never-ending source of speculation to visitors. Although the municipality felt that an opera season gave the town prestige, they were not prepared to spend much money on it: in fact, in 1913 it was to consist of two performances each of *Lakmé*, *Madame Butterfly* and *Carmen* crammed into a fortnight at the end of the season, following a succession of frivolous touring operettes which were deemed to be more to the taste of High Season holidaymakers.

As to engage an opera company of repute would have been outrageously expensive, the method chosen was to cast each opera with principals who already knew the rôles, rehearse a chorus recruited from local enthusiasts, and augment the operette orchestra with instrumentalists from the school of music. Scenery could always be improvised from what had been held in stock, since time immemorial, in a storeroom under the stage.

13

The scenery in question consisted of two sets, one which sufficed for indoor scenes of all periods, and one which gave an approximation of the outdoors. For greater variety, the sets were occasionally re-painted, and so great a thickness of paint had accrued through the years that the flats were very heavy to shift.

There are three settings in *Lakmé*: the garden before an Indian temple, a market place, and a clearing in a forest. They presented no problems: a dark green backcloth with a foreground of potted palms from the casino tearoom would do basically for Acts I and III, while the witch's hut, left over from a long-forgotten production of *Hansel and Gretel* would do, if set at different angles, for both the temple and the market hall.

It would be the first time that the noted soprano Ernestine Thibault, of the Opéra-Comique, who was to sing the title-rôles in both *Lakmé* and *Madame Butterfly*, had graced these boards, and there was every possibility of a faint glimmer of interest among the population.

The artistic director, Maurice Blanc, late of the Opéra Municipal, Fécamp, called the electrician and gave him detailed instructions for the lighting: 'Not too bright for the first act, very bright for the second, and gloomy for the third.'

The musical director, Guillaume Rochebrun, who also directed the town band, mounted the podium and extended a hand across the balustrade to shake that of Monsieur Blanc, who was seated in the front row of the stalls. 'A great and popular work, Monsieur Blanc,' he said, 'and my piano rehearsal this morning assured me that it will be finely sung.' He turned to placate a clarinettist to whom the bassoon part of *The Tales of Hoffman* had been distributed in error. There was a crash behind the curtain as the temple fell over.

Monsieur Blanc was anxious to start the rehearsal. He knew that the costumes which had been put in the dressing-rooms were far from ideal, and he expected protests from the performers – but the costumes had done service for many operas in the past, and there seemed no reason why they should not do for this one.

The bass who was to sing the rôle of Milakantha, Brahmin priest and father of the eponymous heroine, stuck his head through the curtains, and Monsieur Blanc hastened to get the first word in. 'I know it's not very authentic, but when it's lit that costume looks magnificent, and the helmet makes you look taller.'

'I'm quite tall enough for this company,' said the bass, scornfully.

'There are more serious things than this diabolical costume: we have no Lakmé.'

'Isn't Ernestine there?'

'No, she isn't, and one of the chorus has just come in with a story that she was seen being taken into the commissariat, handcuffed to a cop.'

'Handcuffed?'

'Apparently there's been a murder.'

Monsieur Blanc turned and ran up the gangway in the dark auditorium, cursing as he caught his thighs on the *strapontins*. Bursting into the foyer, he ran upstairs to the office of the manager, Monsieur Drach, who doubled as advertising director of the local newspaper, which was popularly known as the One Minute Silence, because that was the average time it took to read it. Drach was just leaving his office in rather a hurry, as he had remembered that he had ordered no programmes for the following evening's performance, and to have left it so late meant that there would be black ink on many pairs of white gloves ... but one couldn't think of everything, even though one drew a small percentage on the cost of the printing, which was done at the newspaper office. Monsieur Blanc and Monsieur Drach collided.

'I must use your telephone. We have a crisis on our hands.'

'Another? What is it this afternoon?'

'Ernestine Thibault isn't here. There's been a murder.'

'I'm not surprised. When I heard her F-sharp at this morning's rehearsal, I said to myself ...'

'She seems to have done the murdering: she's been arrested.' He was at the telephone, turning the handle. 'The commissariat, please ... No, I don't know the number: you'll have to look it up.'

'After you with that telephone,' said Monsieur Drach, 'I must give this to the newspaper.'

An elderly female chorister, dressed in a gipsy costume from *Il Trovatore*, came breathlessly into the office. 'The curtain will go up,' she declaimed dramatically. 'I can sing Lakmé. I've sung it in Yvetot and Creil.'

'Forty-seven years ago, no doubt,' said Monsieur Blanc, cruelly. 'If we're reduced to gipsy costumes for the priestesses, tell the wardrobe mistress to give you one of the *Carmen* ones; they're more eastern.' He shook the telephone. 'Something's crawled into this thing and died.'

Inspectors Lautier and Verdi had assembled Madame Berthier, Madame Masson and Monsieur Peyronnet in Bonpain's office. Of his working garbs, Monsieur Peyronnet had decided that his waiter's suit was the more suitable for such a formal occasion. As the commissaire entered, the telephone rang. He picked up the receiver.

'Are you there?' he said. 'Who? ... Yes, Monsieur Blanc, what is it? ... A murder? Another one? ... Ah, that sounds like the same one ... Ernestine who? ... Singing what? ... My dear Monsieur Blanc, I have much on my mind, and I cannot concern myself at the moment with a missing singer ... I have her here? ... Hold the line.' He removed the receiver from his ear and looked at Madame Masson. 'Are you a singer by any chance?'

'I like to think so.'

'Sacred name of a name!' exclaimed Verdi.

'What's the matter Verdi?' asked Bonpain.

Verdi was wide-eyed. He was gazing raptly at Madame Masson. 'Your stage name is Ernestine Thibault. Tomorrow night you are singing Lakmé.'

'I am, if I'm ever let out of this place,' replied the lady.

'I have a ticket for the front row of the second balcony.'

'Is your name really Verdi?'

'It is, and my father comes from Parma, but unhappily he has been unable to trace a family connection with the immortal one.'

Bonpain was not musical, and the brief interchange meant little to him, so he resumed his conversation on the telephone. 'Are you there?'

Monsieur Blanc was indeed there, and he was talking very loudly and very fast.

'No,' said Bonpain. 'The lady certainly can't come to the Opera House. She is a key witness in a serious criminal investigation, and her testimony is vital.'

Monsieur Blanc talked again, louder and faster.

'Whether she can appear at tomorrow evening's performance depends on the results of the investigation, Monsieur Blanc. Good day to you.' Bonpain replaced the receiver and looked at Madame Masson. The only operatic performance he had ever attended was one of *Tosca*, and he could well imagine an opera singer committing murder. 'So you're singing at the Opera House,' he said.

'She's from the Opéra-Comique in Paris,' said Verdi, impressively.

'I don't care for theatrical people,' said Madame Berthier. 'I don't

16

even care for Madame Bernhardt herself. I've had many of them pass through my hands at my establishment, and I can't begin to tell you what they get up to.'

'Murder?' asked Madame Masson politely.

Bonpain consulted the identity papers which had been collected from the Hotel of the Loire and of the Golden Chariot. 'Now, Madame, your full name is Ernestine Jeanne Masson, *née* Thibault, professionally known as Ernestine Thibault.'

'Correct.'

'Is your husband with you?'

'He proved to be a man of unsettled habits; he was last heard of in Madagascar with a lady conjuror.'

'I see.' Bonpain made a note. 'You were born in Dijon on the third of August . . .'

'It isn't necessary to read out the year. Let it suffice that I was born under the sign of Leo.'

'You surprise me, Madame,' said Madame Berthier. 'I had immediately assumed that you were an Aquarian.'

Bonpain rose and walked to the window. *Sergent de Ville* Maupas had posted himself at the entrance to the Berthier establishment and was flirting with two young female holidaymakers with bows on their shoes. Tied to the railings was a crudely lettered notice saying 'Closed'.

'Verdi.'

'*Monsieur le Commissaire?*'

'What time was the murder?'

Verdi consulted his notebook. 'I noticed the commotion at eleven-seventeen. *Sergents de Ville* Bonnet and Lemaître joined me ten minutes later. The hand ambulance removed the body at eleven-forty-eight. I arrested Mademoiselle Thibault at eleven-fifty-eight.' He turned to her, his dark eyes moist with emotion. 'I hope you will forgive me.'

She gave him a forbearing and expansive smile; her bridgework was superb. ' "Forgiveness is the final virtue", as your great namesake put it,' she said.

'*Sicilian Vespers*, the second act duet,' identified Inspector Verdi, happily.

'Lautier,' said Bonpain, to bring himself into the scene again, 'send six men to Madame Berthier's establishment to search for the murder weapon. I want every grain of sand sifted, every duckboard examined closely, and the cabins taken apart.'

Madame Berthier protested that she was being deprived of her livelihood, and Peyronnet saw himself having to exist for several days on his *pourboires* at Le Florida.

'*Monsieur le Commissaire* ...'

'What is it, Lautier? Get on with it, man.'

'It's a question of manpower. We already have nine men checking the hotels to discover the identity of the murdered man, and we have the day-and-night watch at the Grand Hotel of the Baths and of Serbia.'

'Then the men must work longer hours. Remind them that they have the privilege of serving one of the most beautiful and progressive towns in our beautiful and progressive country.'

With a sinking heart, Lautier left to do so.

'Monsieur Peyronnet, you will kindly tell me your version of this morning's events,' said Bonpain.

Except that he put himself firmly in the limelight as a dashing and somewhat heroic figure, Peyronnet's testimony did not differ from those already provided. He was a loquacious man and it was with a sigh of relief that Bonpain turned to Ernestine.

'How long have you been in our town, Madame?'

'Two days.'

'Is that sufficient to rehearse whichever rôle it is you are committed to sing tomorrow night?'

'I have sung the rôle of Lakmé many times before, both in this country and abroad.'

'Abroad?'

'In Belgium.'

'When and how were you offered the engagement?'

'In the early spring, Monsieur Blanc heard me sing Thaïs at St Omer. He came to my dressing-room and, after the customary haggle about money, I accepted the engagement.'

'Had you known Monsieur Blanc before?'

'No.'

'Have you visited this town before?'

'Never.'

'Apart from Monsieur Blanc, did you know anybody else here when you arrived?'

'Two years ago, in Le Tréport, I worked with the tenor who is singing Gerald.'

'Did he go swimming with you this morning?'

'Certainly not.'

'Why are you so emphatic, Madame?'

'Apart from the size of his stomach, he has flat feet and bad breath; it's enough that I have to sing with him.'

'At what hour did you reach the bathing establishment this morning?'

'At about ten o'clock.'

Bonpain looked to Madame Berthier and Monsieur Peyronnet for corroboration. Both nodded.

'You entered the water perhaps a quarter of an hour later?'

'About that.'

'Inspector Verdi noticed the *brouhaha* at the establishment at about eleven-seventeen. You were then in your cabin, dressing.'

'I was.'

'Were you nearly dressed?'

'I believe I mentioned earlier – I was in my drawers.'

Bonpain coughed. 'You needn't be so explicit. What occurs to me is that if you left your cabin at about ten-fifteen and didn't return to it until, say, eleven o'clock, that gives you forty-five minutes to swim. That's a long time.'

'She is a magnificent swimmer,' said Peyronnet, enthusiastically. 'Such power! Such physique! Such endurance!'

'I can imagine Madame as a Rhine Maiden,' said Verdi.

'Wagner makes me vomit,' said Ernestine.

'Me too,' said Verdi, 'but I stand by what I said.'

'Did you speak to anybody on the beach, Madame?' asked Bonpain.

'Certainly not. I ran straight down to the water's edge in my bathing cloak, and ran straight up again when I had finished my bathe. One should not linger on the beach while the sun is shining; it browns the skin.'

' "O fair complexion of white purity", as the tenor sings in *Otello*,' said Verdi.

The telephone bell rang again. Bonpain picked up the receiver. 'Are you there?... You again, Monsieur Blanc? I have to warn you that you're obstructing the path of justice, and... No, I don't know when you can have your soprano back. For all I know, she may go to the guillotine.'

19

'Like Madeleine in *Andrea Chenier*,' said Verdi, emotionally.

Bonpain replaced the receiver. 'It surprises me, Madame, that you have chosen to stay at the Hotel of the Loire and of the Golden Chariot. It's one of our most renowned hotels, and the terms are far from cheap. It's customary for visiting artistes to select somewhere more modest.'

'I've stayed in many good hotels – the Hotel of the Rhone and of Russia, in Lyon, the Hotel of the Bridge and of the Fourth of September, in Avignon, the Hotel of Louis XI and of the Jetty, in Nice: you will find that the bill was paid promptly at all of them.'

Lautier had re-entered the room. 'I have a rich cousin who stayed at the Hotel of Louis XI and of the Jetty,' he said. 'He complained that the breakfast coffee was abominable.'

'And cold,' confirmed Ernestine.

Lautier carried a note, which he put in front of the commissaire. Bonpain read it and his brow furrowed.

'There's no reason why the contents of this note should be confidential,' he said. 'A difficulty has arisen. No person answering to the description of the murdered man is known at any of the hotels in the town.'

'He could have come here for the day,' suggested Peyronnet.

'We don't encourage day trippers,' said Bonpain, sternly. He turned to Lautier. 'He may have been a private guest. Have the men call at every private house in the town and the surrounding area.'

'With nine men, that'll take a long time.'

'Then put fifteen on to it.'

'I've already explained the manpower situation, *Monsieur le Commissaire*.'

'It's your job to bother with the details, Lautier.'

'Very well, *Monsieur le Commissaire*.' Lautier went out again.

'In a few days we shall stage a reconstruction of the crime,' said Bonpain importantly. 'Perhaps next week.'

'After the Wednesday of next week I shall be in Étaples, singing Marguerite in *Faust*,' said Ernestine.

' "Lovelier than the angels thou" ' murmured Verdi. 'It's my favourite aria – from the church scene.'

'There's an octave jump in the seventeenth bar which is a sod.'

'Even Melba can't manage it,' said Verdi, gallantly.

'She's overrated, that one,' said the singer.

'Going back to the subject of expense, Madame,' said Bonpain, 'I notice that your address is, 197, Avenue due Bois-de-Bologne.'

'Correct.'

'I believe I'm right in saying that the Avenue du Bois-de-Boulogne is one of the most expensive streets in Paris.'

'It certainly is, but the apartment is paid for by the gentleman who is – shall I say he is my protector?'

'You are underwritten, Madame?'

'It's not unknown in my profession : in fact, for a young singer it's essential. For the privilege of launching myself in *Lakmé* at the Opéra-Comique, I had to give the management ten thousand francs – and if it had been *Carmen* it would have been thirty thousand.'

'Would you consider it indiscreet, Madame, if I were to ask for the name of your protector?'

'Not at all, *Monsieur le Commissaire*. It's the Minister of Justice.'

'Oh, my God!' moaned Bonpain.

By half past three, Ernestine Thibault was once more rehearsing on the stage of the Opera House, and was just beginning the first act duet with her confidante, Mallika. The priestess in the gipsy costume, feeling that she had been insulted by Monsieur Blanc, had been singing louder than any other chorister and throwing in very high harmonies whenever possible, to show him that he had rejected the loudest and highest Lakmé in the business.

At the commissariat, Bonpain was still interrogating Madame Berthier and Monsieur Peyronnet. Nothing new had been elicited, but as this was the most important case in his career so far, he felt he might as well keep working on the details until more substantial evidence turned up.

Opposite the commissariat, an appreciative crowd had gathered by the promenade railings to watch the search for the murder weapon. Taking Bonpain at his word, each cabin was carried further down the beach to be dismantled methodically, while two *sergents de ville*, on their knees, raked the sand. Each towel was unfolded and shaken, and the mangle, used to squeeze water from bathing costumes, was rendered unusable for evermore when examined by Inspector Boitot, who had no mechanical sense whatever. There was consultation on the possibility of the minute hand of one of the clock faces showing the times of high tides having been used as the weapon, but practical tests showed that neither would pass through the hole in the partition. There were a number of protests from holidaymakers deprived of their afternoon swim, and opposite the Hotel of the White Horse and of the Low Countries a commercial traveller was arrested for undressing on the beach.

Sergent de Ville Maupas had been taken off his duties on the promenade and put among those knocking on the doors of private houses to ask if any male approximating to the description of the murdered man had failed to come home to luncheon. He had been allocated a street inhabited largely by gas works employees, and he had been greeted with angry words, and even threats of violence, by those on the night staff whom he had awakened from their legitimate afternoon slumber.

It was frustrating work, and he was delighted to have an idea which he thought could be to his advantage. All the hotels had been checked that morning and now the private houses were being combed, but he would bet five francs to four that the commissaire had forgotten to order the checking of what could only be described as semi-private houses. What about, for instance, Madame Zizi's establishment, where the red light over the door glowed day and night? What likelier port of call could there be for a wealthy (for rumour had it that the man's clothes were of the best) middle-aged (for so he was described on the piece of paper which Maupas carried) visitor (which he must have been, because nobody had recognized him while he was lying dead on the duckboards)? If he were to bring back the answer to the problem from a quarter which nobody had considered, there could be commendation, or even promotion.

He knocked on Madame Zizi's door. There were sounds of life within, and the mechanical piano was playing. Three-thirty was a time when many housewives went shopping, and on a warm afternoon there would be a temptation for husbands to walk round for a little extra-marital exercise.

The door was opened by a short-skirted maid, a sturdy girl from the Auvergne whose charms were few but who could be relied upon to perform extra duties on occasions when clients outnumbered staff. Maupas saluted smartly. He was not a usual visitor because the good behaviour of the establishment was the responsibility of the Morals Squad, but he had visited the house on a number of occasions, both as a policeman and a private citizen, and he was known to the personnel.

He was received in the salon by Madame Zizi, a neat, ageing little

22

woman in black bombazine who had once been one of the most athletic girls in the profession. Sitting on a banquette in diaphanous negligées were a plump blonde from Picardy, who was knitting a baby garment for a pregnant sister, a brunette from the Dombe, polishing her nails for the fourteenth time that day, and the exotic Miss Barbara, a heavyweight quadroon from the Antilles, reading Kant's *Critique of Pure Reason*.

Madame Zizi switched off the piano and prepared to be co-operative. No, she was sure that, during her hours on duty, no client resembling the murdered man had entered the establishment, and she sent the plump blonde to awaken Mademoiselle Titi, who had been in charge the previous night after she herself had retired. Mademoiselle Titi also professed herself as being unable to help, and Maupas was about to replace his *képi* and depart when Madame Zizi said, with cheerful generosity, 'Surely you needn't rush off. Miss Barbara, take the *sergent de ville* up to the Blue Room for ten minutes.' Turning again to Maupas, she added, 'It will refresh you.'

As she watched the delighted policeman follow the coloured girl out of the door, she reflected that it was always a good thing to keep on the right side of the police, and this method was cheaper than offering a glass of wine.

In spite of Maupas's conjecture, Bonpain had not forgotten the semi-private houses, and he had summoned to his office Inspector Vaquin, who was in charge of the Morals Squad.

'Vaquin,' said the commissaire, 'a wealthy, middle-aged man comes to our town. He is still young enough to make full use of his appetites. He does not stay in a hotel, so it is possible that he makes arrangements of a semi-private nature. Have you any suggestions?'

'Obviously, *Monsieur le Commissaire*, there is the establishment of Madame Zizi.'

'And the others?'

'Apart from Madame Zizi's which, as you know, is officially recognized and regularly inspected, there are at the moment three clandestine establishments.'

'That seems too many, Vaquin. A little unofficial competition is good for any enterprise, but three seems a lot. There is Widow Leroux's, of course.'

Widow Leroux's was a sleazy establishment by the port which catered for a low class of trade. For many years the police had turned a blind eye to its activities because it was a useful gathering place of army deserters, runaway seamen, and minor villains of many varieties. The women employed there, believed to be relatives of the widow herself, would be touched with a bargepole only by those who were singularly drunk or desperate.

Both Bonpain and Vaquin smiled and shook their heads. No man with money in his pocket would spend two minutes at the Widow's, let alone spend a night there.

'There are the Granval Sisters,' suggested Vaquin.

'Who?'

'It's a very small, very special establishment consisting only of the two young ladies themselves. They are twins and they work as a team, if you understand me. As you will appreciate, it is a very exotic and a very rare offering, and therefore very costly.'

'I'm sure of it,' said Bonpain. Reflectively, he added, 'I think it's a very healthy sign that the town now has sufficient reputation to be able to attract that kind of speciality.'

'I agree. For that reason we've never worried the girls, apart from keeping a benevolent and watchful eye on them.'

'Quite right,' said Bonpain. 'And in the present instance they may well be helpful.'

'I'm afraid not. Unfortunately, they left two days ago for a visit to Rome with a wealthy American.'

'That's that, then.' As an afterthought, Bonpain asked: 'Real sisters?'

'No doubt about it, we've checked their papers. Born in Grenoble and convent educated.'

'And the third clandestine establishment?'

'It's known as Cousin Emile's. It does us little credit, and we have it marked down for a visit in force as soon as a propitious evening presents itself.'

'Why must you choose your evening so carefully?'

'It caters for the more depressing perversions, and I regret to say that it's frequented by many of our most prominent citizens. It would hardly be a good idea to raid it on an evening when the mayor is there.'

Bonpain wasn't so sure about that, but he thought his view might be a personal one so he didn't express it. 'Madame Zizi's, together with the two operating clandestine establishments, must be checked at once for traces of the murdered man,' he said.

'At once, *Monsieur le Commissaire*.'

'And obviously you have a list of those ladies of comparatively easy virtue who will oblige a lonely gentleman of independent means.'

'We keep the list carefully up to date, and they will be visited immediately.'

'There are also a number of cafés which . . .'

'They, too, will be covered most thoroughly. Of course, last night the Opera House was closed, so we don't have to worry about that.'

'The Opera House? What's the Opera House to do with it?'

'For many years it has been a *théâtre à femmes*. Hasn't *Monsieur le Commissaire* noticed?'

'I'm not an opera-goer. Explain.'

'The intervals are long, so notes may be sent to women displaying themselves in the boxes and assignations made.'

'Well, I'm damned, I didn't know that was going on.'

'It's very harmless, *Monsieur le Commissaire*.'

'Whose little business is it – the manager's?'

'There's a small charge to the women in question. Monsieur Drach shares it with the woman in the box-office.'

'Vaquin, everybody in this town makes money except me.'

'Yes, *Monsieur le Commissaire*.'

At the Grand Hotel of the Baths and of Serbia, the doorman saluted as the white-haired, red-faced Colonel Arbuthnot Withers swaggered into the lobby.

Grunwald, the man from Paris, hurried across to greet him. 'Colonel,' he said, 'you've given me seventeen heart attacks.' He was a small and dapper man, with large, sad brown eyes. 'It was unkind of you both to leave the hotel without telling me where you were going.'

The colonel grinned and laid a forefinger to his lips. 'Affair of the heart, my dear fellow. Discretion and all that. Eh, what?'

Grunwald lowered his voice, looking over the colonel's shoulder. 'Where is His Majesty?'

'Haven't the vaguest, old boy.'

'He's not with you?'

'Good heavens, no. Three's a crowd, and all that. Eh, what?'

'Where is he, for God's sake?' Grunwald's face was white.

'I've just told you, I don't know. We had a little conference last night: I told him I had this rather good address which a feller in the

In-and-Out gave me before I left London, and HM said he had a little deal on too – and we both stole out the back way soon after ten-thirty.'

'In which direction did he go?'

'He wandered off along the prom, old boy.'

Grunwald ran across to the reception desk, where Inspector Léonard Hanoteau was still on duty. 'HM?' he asked, breathlessly.

'Presumably still in his room, Monsieur Grunwald. He hasn't come down all day.'

'Oh, yes, he has; he went out the back way with Colonel Withers at about ten-thirty.' He knew that, when he was excited, he spoke with a slight lisp.

'He certainly didn't come through the lobby, Monsieur Grunwald. Colonel Withers has just come in.'

'I know, I've just spoken to him.'

'So I noticed. As they've been out together, doesn't the colonel know where he is?'

'They parted on the promenade when they left.'

'My colleague, Inspector Gibeau, is responsible for watching the exterior of the hotel, Monsieur Grunwald.'

Grunwald shot out of the front entrance, almost overturning an elderly Swedish countess, who was going out in a more leisurely manner. Where was Gibeau? He ran down the steps and along the pavement to the corner, and looked along the frontage which faced the sea. There was no Gibeau. He ran back past the front entrance and along to the alley which led to the staff entrance. In an angle of the wall stood Gibeau, with a wine bottle to his lips. When he saw Grunwald, he hastily replaced the bottle in its hiding place behind a dustbin, and hastened towards him.

'Everything all right, Monsieur Grunwald?'

'Did you see HM and Colonel Withers leave the hotel by the back way this morning?'

'No. Should I have?'

'You didn't see them go down to the promenade together at about half past ten, and then separate?

'No.'

'Did you see Colonel Withers return on his own just now?'

Gibeau considered. It occurred to him that he ought to be able to give the right answer, but it was a hot day and the bottle behind the dustbin was not the first. He had to admit to himself that his wits were not at their sharpest.

Grunwald lost patience, waiting for him to speak. 'I shall report your flagrant dereliction of duty to Commissaire Bonpain, and I suggest you start looking for alternative employment.' He ran back into the hotel.

Miserably, Gibeau went back to his bottle. How the hell could they expect you to keep observation without a bottle? What did 'dereliction' mean? Why was everybody so unreasonable?

In the foyer, Colonel Withers was at the flower stall, patting the arm of the sales-girl. Grunwald took him aside. 'Are you quite sure you don't know where His Majesty went?'

'Quite sure, dear boy.'

'He gave you no indication?'

'None at all, and neither did I give him any indication of what I was up to. When a lady's name is involved, one keeps mum, what?'

'I believe this is not the first unofficial holiday on which you have accompanied His Majesty.'

'Indeed no, old sport. Dammit, we were at Harrow together. There's none of that "King" nonsense when he's with me, you know.'

'Would you be kind enough to tell me, Colonel, in the strictest confidence, something of His Majesty's proclivities.'

'That's a long word, dear fellow. I think you'll have to explain.'

'What are His Majesty's special interests – sexually, I mean.'

'Women, I suppose. Rather obvious, isn't it, old man?'

'But does he like them large or small, old or young, dark or fair? Has he any special desires, such as being tied up or beaten?'

'Tied up or beaten, old man? You must be out of your mind. Who on earth would want to be tied up or beaten? Jolly painful, if you ask me. Most unpleasant. I'll tell you what, I think you've got rather a dirty mind, old man. Let's change the subject, shall we?' He shook off Grunwald's restraining hand and went back to the flower stall.

Grunwald shot back to Inspector Hanoteau. 'Telephone me urgently at the commissariat if anything happens,' he commanded.

'What in particular are you expecting to happen, Monsieur?'

'Anything.'

Grunwald sped out of the front door again, almost overturning the elderly Swedish countess, who was returning for her parasol. In the road stood a row of open taxis, each with a white canopy edged with a silken fringe. He jumped into the first. 'To the commissariat!' he shouted.

The hall porter was standing on the steps, crimson with anger. If a guest required a taxi, it was his duty to open the door, instruct the driver where to go and accept a tip.

The driver sneered. The idle rich! Fancy taking a cab for the few hundred metres to the commissariat! Anyway, by the time he got his engine going, and had proceeded at the eight kilometres an hour which was the speed limit along the promenade, his fare would have been able to walk to the commissariat and back again four times.

The Morals Squad van, in which so many ladies of the *demi-monde* had shouted and bawled and banged on the tin walls, eructated to a halt outside Madame Zizi's. Inspector Vaquin climbed out, followed by two of his men. They were intelligent, alert young men, because every member of the force wanted to get into the Morals Squad, and Vaquin had the pick of the best.

This was a murder investigation, and Vaquin had a sense of drama. He pushed past the short-skirted maid from the Auvergne and strode into the salon. With a sigh, Madame Zizi again switched off the mechanical piano. It seemed to be raining policemen.

'How many girls on duty?' Vaquin snapped curtly.

Madame Zizi waved in the direction of the plump blonde from Picardy and the brunette from the Dombe, both of whom beamed and nodded.

'And upstairs?'

'Three.'

Vaquin turned to his two *sergents de ville*. 'Have them down – and whoever's with them.'

The two men ran for the door. 'But don't disturb Mademoiselle Titi,' Madame Zizi called after them. 'She's in the yellow room, and she needs her sleep.' She turned back to Vaquin. 'Is there anything especially wrong?' she asked.

'Murder,' Vaquin squared his jaw.

'*Tiens, tiens,*' murmured Madame Zizi, while the two girls on the banquette opened their eyes wide in horror. 'Murder is something we take very seriously in our profession. It's a national disgrace, the number of us who are done to death. In recent years, it has become an occupational hazard.'

There was a clatter of footsteps on the stairs, and the *sergents de ville* chased in a party of six: there were three girls in half-adjusted peignoirs, one of whom was the brown-skinned Barbara, and three gentlemen buttoning their trousers, one of whom was Maupas.

'You!' said Inspector Vaquin.

'I can explain everything, *Monsieur l'Inspecteur*,' said Maupas, struggling with a recalcitrant fly-button. 'It was in the cause of duty.'

It was very warm in Bonpain's office, and the rate of questioning had slowed down. Lautier had his left elbow on his desk and his chin resting in his cupped hand: every now and then he dozed off and his chin slid out of the cup, so that he started awake.

The door flew open, and Grunwald rushed in, followed by a startled *sergent de ville* whose job was to stop people rushing in.

'*Monsieur le Commissaire* . . .'

'My dear Monsieur Grunwald . . .'

'Kindly get these people out of here at once. I must speak to you most urgently.'

'Monsieur Grunwald, I'm engaged in a criminal investigation of the highest importance.'

'The matter on which I have to speak to you is of even greater importance.'

'I think that is for me to judge.'

'I have already had to tell your Inspector Gibeau that he will be well advised to start looking for alternative employment.'

'The devil you have!'

'I repeat, *Monsieur le Commissaire*, get these people out of here and give me your undivided attention – or I cannot be answerable for the consequences.'

Impressed, Bonpain waved out Inspectors Verdi and Lautier, and the witnesses, Madame Berthier and Monsieur Peyronnet.

The telephone rang. Bonpain answered it. 'Are you there?' He listened for a moment, and passed the instrument to Grunwald. 'For you.'

Grunwald took the receiver. 'Grunwald.'

It was Inspector Hanoteau. 'You said I was to telephone you if anything happened.'

'Yes, yes, I did.'

'The girl from the flower stall has pushed Colonel Withers into the fountain.'

'Idiot!' said Grunwald, slamming down the receiver.

'May I now know what the excitement is about?' asked Bonpain. Grunwald took a deep breath. 'HM has disappeared.'

'Since when?'

'Since about half past ten this morning.'

'That's not very long.'

'It could be long enough.'

'And our precautions ... ?'

'... were useless.'

'He's probably perfectly all right somewhere.'

'But where? It's our job to know where. If they get to know in Paris that he's been wandering about without surveillance, we'll both be unemployed in the morning.'

'Then we must look for him,' said Bonpain, thinking ruefully of the manpower situation.

'Exactly. I want thirty men at once.'

'Thirty, my dear Grunwald?'

'Either I get them from you or I get them from the Minister of the Interior.'

Only an hour or so earlier, Bonpain had been involved, at a short remove, with the Minister of Justice. Two ministers in a day were too many. 'I'll do what I can,' he said. 'Tell me what you know.'

Grunwald told him. It did not take long.

'The likelihood is that he's in someone's bed,' said Bonpain. 'Fortuitously, in connection with another investigation, every house of assignation has been – or is being – searched; every amenable woman is being questioned.'

'Let me emphasize that apart from our own personal well-being, the equilibrium of Europe rests on His Majesty's safety. It's vital, for all our sakes, to know in *whose* bed. It's in bed that the most dangerous ideas are exchanged. He could be in bed with a female socialist.'

'Such people are not made welcome in our town, Monsieur Grunwald.' He pushed a pad and a pencil across the desk. 'Although a description has naturally been issued to those members of my staff who are guarding him, it would be advantageous to have one as complete as possible.'

As he watched Grunwald propel the pencil across the paper, he had the first premonition. He could see the words forming upside down: 'His Majesty is a man of middle years; he has a round face with pale complexion and a small moustache ...'

A cold chill struck Bonpain in the depths of his stomach. 'I regret, Monsieur Grunwald, it is not necessary to write any more. I know where His Majesty is.'

The pencil stopped.

'You know? Where?'

'In the cellar beneath the fish market.'

'The cellar . . . ?'

'In this hot weather, it is the only place to put them.'

'You mean His Majesty is dead?'

'Yes, Monsieur Grunwald.'

Grunwald grabbed the telephone. 'Get me the Ministry of Foreign Affairs immediately. I wish to speak to the minister himself.'

Bonpain gulped. Three ministers in a day. It could be a record.

The minister was not free to take Grunwald's call, so it was taken by his *chef de cabinet*, the tall, distinguished, silver-haired Charles Lavigny.

The minister was having a singularly boring afternoon. The curtains in his office had been drawn and he was being given a magic lantern lecture. There was this Intelligence officer who had returned from somewhere on the Baltic Sea, and he was projecting photographic slides of assemblies of German battleships. To the minister, one battleship looked just like another, and the showing had gone on far too long. He really did not see what the Intelligence officer was getting so worked up about: it was common knowledge that Germany had a fleet – most countries had one – and the discovery that the German fleet appeared to be bigger than had been presumed didn't seem very important. After all, if the Germans wanted to spend their money on extra battleships instead of more frivolous items such as fashion and fine foods, it was entirely their own affair. He wished he had never been put into this job because, before the last Cabinet reshuffle, he had been perfectly happy as Minister of Physical Culture, which had involved attending fascinating gymnastic displays, often by females.

He was very glad when Charles Lavigny hurried in and turned the lights on. 'Forgive me, *Monsieur le Ministre*,' he said, as he hurried across the room, picking his way among the boxes in which the Intelligence officer's magic lantern apparatus had been delivered. 'Something of the utmost importance.'

'There is, eh?' said the minister, rising to his feet and stretching.

'Then you'd better go,' he said to the Intelligence officer, adding, 'It's all been very interesting,' so as not to offend the fellow too much.

'I've only another dozen or two more slides to show,' said the officer, with a note of desperation. He had been trying to reach the minister's eyes and ears for months.

'Some other time, then.' Turning to Lavigny, the minister said: 'Find somebody to whom this gentleman can show his slides.'

'Certainly, *Monsieur le Ministre*,' said Lavigny, taking the Intelligence officer by the elbow and pushing him towards the door.

'Isn't he going to take all his stuff?' asked the minister, as Lavigny courteously eased the visitor out into the passage.

'Something dreadful has happened.'

'He can't possibly leave it all here.'

'It's the King of Mittenstein-Hoffnung.'

'Somebody's going to fall over it.'

'He's been assassinated on French soil.'

'If the fellow doesn't want the stuff, send it to the Admiralty; it's a lot of battleships.'

'*Monsieur le Ministre*, this is vital and immediate.'

'If somebody's been assassinated, it's not our pigeon. It's either Justice or the Interior; I can never remember which of them looks after the police.'

'This is not a police matter; this is diplomatic.'

'Who did you say it was?'

'The King of Mittenstein-Hoffnung.'

'Show me on the map.'

Picking his way among the boxes, Lavigny pulled down a wall map. He stabbed a finger in an area to the east of France.

'It's not very big,' said the minister.

'Remarkably small, really.'

'Why a king then? I should have thought a grand duke would be sufficient.'

'That was Napoleon's doing. In return for the grand duke's support he made him a king. Then the new king lost forty thousand of his subjects on the retreat from Moscow, so it was an expensive promotion.'

'You wouldn't think there'd be room for forty thousand.'

'The country supplies sixty-three and two-thirds percent of Europe's cauxite.'

'And that's useful stuff, eh?'

32

'Very, if there's a war. When this gets out, the chancelleries of Europe will be aflame.'

'Then it had better not get out until we've thought what to do.'

'That was the procedure I was going to recommend.'

'So what do we do?'

'I suggest we send our best investigator – and there is only one man in France.'

'Picard?'

'Exactly.'

'Is he free?'

'He can be made free.' He pulled down another wall map, and indicated a coastal town. 'That is where he must go.'

'I like that place. You don't think I'd better go myself?'

'*Monsieur le Ministre* could not leave Paris without his absence being noted.'

'I suppose you're right. That's all we can do then.'

'For the moment, *Monsieur le Ministre*.'

'Other than getting these boxes cleared out.'

Tuesday, 9 September

At two o'clock the following afternoon, Chanteloup Picard entered a first-class non-smoking compartment of a train from Paris, followed by a porter carrying two suitcases and an attaché case.

'When you have disposed of the baggage, you will kindly stand in the doorway and ensure that no other passengers come in,' said Picard. He had been despatched on this investigation at a few hours notice, and there had been no time to reserve a compartment.

Having put the suitcases on the rack and the attaché case on the seat, the porter extended his hand, palm upwards.

'When the train goes,' said Picard firmly. He flicked a speck of dust from his sleeve and settled himself in a corner seat with his back to the engine. It was less pleasant than riding facing the engine, but in that position one risked unsightly smuts of soot on one's face, together with the possibility of various bronchial and catarrhal ailments occasioned by draughts.

He was a tall, good-looking man, with regular features and a thick crop of brown hair brushed back from his forehead. He wore a black jacket with carefully-cut striped trousers, and a grey trilby hat. In his buttonhole was the thin puce ribbon of a decoration seldom awarded to a man still in his thirties.

When the whistle blew, Picard slipped a coin into the hand of the porter, whose scowling face had deterred from entering two members of the landed gentry, three ladies of uncertain age and a Turkish dealer in fake Thracian antiquities. As the train rumbled into motion, Picard rose to his feet, opened a window, extracted a duster from his attaché case and briskly dusted all available ledges and crevices. That done, he shook the duster out of the window. The less dust one breathes into one's lungs, he believed, the less exposed one is to any risk of infection.

He sat down again in his corner, took an envelope from his inside breast pocket and broke the wax seal. After his last assignment, he would have welcomed a day or two of leisure; however, an early telephone call to his apartment had brought him instructions to take the train he was on, and a messenger had delivered the sealed orders he was to peruse as soon as the train started. There was little to satisfy his curiosity: on a single sheet of paper was typed 'You will proceed to your destination, where a room has been reserved for you at the Grand Hotel of the Baths and of Serbia. You will unlock the drawer of the bedside cabinet with the enclosed key, and you will find further instructions therein.'

There was nothing more to be done for the next three or four hours so, having torn the piece of paper into tiny fragments and scattered them out of the window, he settled down to read a scandalous new novel by Colette Willy. An investigation at a pleasant French seaside resort was much to his taste after such recent assignments as stirring up industrial unrest in Zagreb, unmasking six Austro-Hungarian secret agents in Dakar, and arranging the kidnapping of an Armenian actress who was blackmailing the President of the Republic.

His satisfaction did not last long. He arrived at the end of the line in pouring rain and had to queue for twenty minutes before being conveyed in a very smelly horse-drawn cab to the hotel, where he found that the room reserved for him was at the back of the building with a view of hundreds of wet roofs, beyond which the gasworks loomed out of the mist. His feelings towards the office staff in Paris were further jaundiced by the discovery that he had been given the wrong key. Having broken the blade of his pocket knife, as well as an ivory shoehorn, in trying vainly to open the drawer in the bedside cabinet, he was forced to prowl the corridors in search of a suitable tool, eventually finding a plasterer's trowel which had been abandoned in a cupboard and which opened the drawer at the cost of a nasty cut to his left thumb. He always worried about injuries to a thumb, because he had once been told that they could lead to lockjaw.

His further instructions read: 'You will be given details of your assignment by Monsieur Grunwald. Act with extreme discretion: the peace of Europe could be in your hands. Due to the importance of the investigation, you may incur expenses on Scale 1A.'

The last sentence raised his spirits, and he went down to the recep-

35

tion desk and demanded a front room: now that the secret, such as it was, had been extracted from the drawer, there seemed no further need to stay in what he could only consider as servants' quarters. He also ordered a bottle of champagne, some toast and caviar, and someone to dust his new room and make sure that new white lining paper was in the drawers.

He sat at the window and watched it rain on the sea. Slowly, darkness crept under the lowering storm clouds. He had just finished the bottle when there was a gentle rap on the door. He opened it to an angry and embittered man with a tie awry and a tear in the knee of his left trouser leg.

'Monsieur Picard?'

'Yes?'

'Grunwald.'

'I was expecting you.'

'You're in the wrong room.'

'I think it more likely that I was in the wrong room in the first place. I am not accustomed to wet gasworks.'

'That room was given to you so that I could climb an easily ascendable drainpipe and make your acquaintance in secret.'

Picard looked at Grunwald's torn trouser leg. 'Easily ascendable?'

'The rain had made it slippery. It was only on the fourth attempt that I reached the window-sill – to find the room unoccupied.'

'I regret the inconvenience to which you were put.'

'Is that bottle empty?'

'I'm afraid so. Are you attached to my department?'

'Yes, I am. In a junior capacity, of course. May I ask what expenses scale you're on?'

'1A.'

'Then do you think you can buy another bottle?'

'Perhaps. Tell me what my assignment is.'

Grunwald tiptoed to the door, opened it suddenly, and looked out into the corridor. Then he looked under the bed, and finally made sure that nobody was clinging to the underside of the balcony.

'It's the King of Mittenstein-Hoffnung,' he said, in a low voice.

'Oh, is it?' Picard's voice expressed disappointment. 'A tiresome man. Whose wife has he knocked up this time?'

'He's been done in.'

'That could present complications.'

'It completely buggers the balance of power in Europe.'

36

'Was no one from our department guarding him?'

'Yes,' said Grunwald. 'I was.'

'Oh.' There was a short pause. 'Who did it? Or is it my assignment to find out?'

'It's your assignment.'

'When did it happen?'

'Yesterday morning.'

'Where?'

'In a bathing cabin – and "Why?" is the other half of the assignment.'

'Thank you,' said Picard.

In a few sentences, Grunwald filled in all the details he knew.

'Who else knows the identity of the murdered man?' asked Picard.

'Only the local commissaire of police – apart from the Paris people, whom I notified in code E.'

'Have there been any known anarchists in town?'

'No. At my suggestion, the commissaire still has his men calling at every house to try to find out who the dead man is.'

'But, for God's sake, we know who the dead man is.'

'It might be a good idea not to let the killer know that we do.'

Picard grunted. He felt that by not immediately tumbling to the ruse he had allowed himself to be outsmarted.

'What sort of a man is the commissaire?'

'His name is Bonpain, and he's bewildered. As he was jointly responsible for safeguarding HM, he's worried about losing his job.'

'As doubtless you are.'

'You could say that.'

'When do I meet the commissaire?'

'In a few minutes.'

'I trust he's not coming here; it's important to maintain an illusion that nothing special is going on.'

'I've invented a cover story that you're a friend of the commissaire's brother-in-law, who lives in Paris. You call to take the commissaire out for a drink.'

'Do I call for him at the commissariat?'

'No, no – at the fish market.'

'The fish market?'

'Yes.'

'It'll be closed by now.'

'It will, but you'll see a barred gate in the wall, next to a pissoir.

It will open to your touch. Inside, you'll see a flight of stairs going down.' He looked at his watch. 'It's time you went. You should be there by nine-thirty.'

'Would it be so awful if I kept the commissaire waiting?'

'It's not that; it's just that you should be there before the post mortem starts.'

'The post mortem?'

'I think you should see the body before the police surgeon cuts it about.'

'You are permitting a post mortem?' Anger and disbelief alternated on Picard's face.

'The commissaire insists. He says that if he doesn't know the cause of death, he can't be expected to solve the problem of who did the murder.'

'I shall solve the problem of who did the murder.'

'Of course, the police surgeon doesn't know the identity of the man he's cutting up.'

'Grunwald, you are a vulva. Do you realize what it would mean if the smallest cut were made on His Majesty's body? It would be lèse-majesté.'

'I suppose you're right. I can't think of everything.'

'Pass me my hat.'

'Shall I wait here until you return?'

'No, I think the less you have to do with this case the better; I'm very unimpressed with your performance so far.' He put on his hat and coat, seized his umbrella and went to the door. 'Do I understand that the post mortem is being held in the fish market?'

'That's right.'

'On second thoughts, you'd better wait in this room.' He went out and ran downstairs. At the front entrance, the porter was huddled under the portico. The rain was coming down in sheets.

'A taxi,' commanded Picard.

'You won't get a taxi tonight, M'sieur – not in rain like this.'

'It's in rain like this that one needs a taxi.'

'But the taxi-drivers don't like water getting in the engine.'

'I can get a taxi when it's raining in Paris.'

'In Paris, it's a different sort of life, M'sieur – and the roads are better.'

'A horse cab then.'

'The drivers here have more consideration for their horses, M'sieur.'

'I have no time to argue; how do I get to the fish market?'

'The grill room is still open, M'sieur.'

'I don't want the grill room, I want the fish market.'

'As M'sieur pleases. Go along the promenade, past the casino, turn right, take the second left beside the Bank of Commerce and the African Colonies, cross the square and take the turning beside the post office. You can't miss it.'

Cursing fluently and inventively, Picard put up his umbrella and sloshed off through the rain. Despite the porter's statement, he found that he could miss it quite easily, and he lost himself in a maze of deserted streets surrounding a large Gothic church which, to judge from the dents in the facades of the surrounding houses and the piles of broken brickwork stacked around its base, was in an advanced state of disrepair.

Turning a corner, he came across a party of police working along a street, calling at every house. One of the men flashed a lantern in his face and asked if he were looking for a missing friend who had a moustache. When Picard said no, he turned away disinterestedly, but Picard seized him by the sleeve and asked the way to the fish market. His watch told him that it was only three minutes before the half-hour.

The cobbles surrounding the fish market were greasy, and the whole area stank. He found the barred gate next to the pissoir and pushed at it gingerly with the ferule of his umbrella. It swung open on noisy hinges. At the bottom of the dark, wet stairs an oil lamp flickered. Cautiously, he descended. It could not be easy to carry bodies up and down such steep and narrow stairs.

A few paces brought him to an archway revealing a scene on which Goya would have pounced with delight. A single gas mantle in the whitewashed ceiling shone down on the naked, ivory-coloured, stiffened, paunchy corpse of His late Majesty of Mittenstein-Hoffnung extended on a rickety table scored by the knives of generations of fish-gutters. Scalpel in hand, a thin, high-cheekboned man with a long grey beard was leaning over the body. In the background, a pimply-faced youth held a box of surgical instruments and a grubby towel. From the shadows stepped forward an authoritative figure whom Picard took to be Commissaire Bonpain.

'You must be the friend of my brother-in-law who lives in Paris,' said the authoritative figure. 'It's nice of you to call. In a few minutes, we'll go for a drink together at the Café des Colonnes. Your name, if I remember rightly, is Monsieur Picard.'

'Chanteloup Picard.' He bowed slightly.

'Let me present the good Doctor Perchepied.'

The bearded man transferred the scalpel from his right to his left hand, and proffered the empty one to Picard. It was as cold as a tomb.

'Have you ever seen a post mortem?' asked Bonpain, chattily. 'It's a fascinating sight when it's performed by a hand as dextrous as that of Doctor Perchepied. A single cut from the chin to the genitals, followed by a few snips with the rib-cutters, and the body is wide open to inspection.'

'Fascinating,' murmured Picard. His mind was racing. During his hurried approach through the rain-soaked streets, he had had no opportunity to plan his next move, which was to call a halt to this surgical performance without arousing any untoward suspicions.

'This is a man who died on the beach today from a wound in the head,' said Bonpain, waving Picard forward. 'Perhaps you'd care to look at him.' In his mind, he was already reading the letter of commendation which this distinguished visitor from Paris would be sending to his superiors at the conclusion of a successful investigation, a letter so glowing that nobody would remember Bonpain's failure to safeguard the king while he was alive.

Forcing down a feeling of revulsion, Picard stepped forward. Between the royal right eye and the bridge of the nose was a small indented wound, surrounded by a purplish bruise. The bearded doctor was already shuffling his feet impatiently, tapping his twenty-centimetre scalpel on a gold ring which he wore on his left hand. He was thinking of a warm fire and a glass of calvados. The pimply-faced youth was thinking of a girl named Estelle.

Picard reviewed the alternatives open to him. He could, of course, reveal his identity and command that the surgery should not take place, but Dr Perchepied was old and probably garrulous, and his assistant was young and almost certainly eager to impress his friends, and therefore both were security risks. Or he could take Bonpain aside and issue urgent instructions to him, but he knew that as soon as he moved out of the way the doctor's scalpel would sweep down upon the royal corpse. Or suppose he were to faint: would that hold up the proceedings? Yes, but not for more than five minutes. These were professionals, who would feel no more than mild amusement at one so queasy at the prospect of seeing human insides. Perhaps, if he feigned madness and attacked the boy ... but the boy was expendable and could be done without.

So it would have to be the doctor. Reaching forward with his left hand, he murmured, 'Pardon me,' and took the scalpel from him while, with the right hand, he swung a blow at the bearded chin, knocking the man flat on his back on the muddy and fish-scaled floor. It was against Picard's better instincts to hit a man of so many years, but he prided himself that he had judged the blow well and, while not hard enough to do serious damage, it had certainly put paid to any professional endeavours for some hours to come.

The boy dropped the box of instruments. Bonpain raised his two hands to his lips with a startled cry of 'Zut!' It was not the reaction for which Picard would have hoped from a commissaire on whom he would have to rely for support : he would have preferred a stronger man.

For the boy's benefit, Picard put on a performance. 'Oh, no!' he shouted. 'I've done it again! This crazy instinct for violence, of which I am so ashamed and which has been with me since childhood, has caused me, once again, to strike an innocent and defenceless person. It is a private madness against which I have fought all my life.' Turning to Bonpain, he added: 'I expect your brother-in-law has warned you about me.'

'Er – no. I mean, yes,' stammered Bonpain.

'Really,' said Picard to himself, 'this commissaire is not good enough.' Then, *sotto voce*, he said : 'Get that young idiot out of here. I must talk to you.'

'Young man,' said Bonpain obediently, 'Leave us. I will look after this situation.'

'The instruments ...' began the boy.

'Dr Perchepied will look after those.'

'When he feels a little better,' added Picard.

The boy took a frightened look at the doctor, who was lying peaceably with his head in a fish basket, and fled.

'There are certain things,' said Picard, 'which we shall have to discuss.'

Picard signalled to the waiter to bring two more glasses of cognac and some more hot coffee. It was approaching midnight. He and

Bonpain had had a useful ninety minutes of conversation, as well as a reasonable meal.

Dr Perchepied had come round quickly and had been driven home in a police conveyance. He was, predictably, suffering from a sore jaw, toothache and a headache, but Bonpain had taken some of the discomfort from his hurts by telling him that his brother-in-law's friend was a rich man who invariably made generous settlements with those whom he hit while suffering from one of his unfortunate brainstorms. ('If the department won't cough up,' said Picard, 'then we'll have to slip him a bit out of the expense account.')

Despite the lateness of the hour, the Café des Colonnes was doing good business. 'Who are all these people coming in?' asked Picard.

'They're from the Opera House,' replied Bonpain. 'They come in here for a nightcap and to pull the performance to pieces.' He thought it unnecessary to inform Picard that one of his men had, on the previous morning, put handcuffs on the opera-singing mistress of the Minister of Justice.

'When are you planning to stage a reconstruction of the crime, *Monsieur le Commissaire*?'

'As soon as we have been able to trace all the participants, Monsieur Picard.'

'Let it be tomorrow, *Monsieur le Commissaire*.'

'Tomorrow?'

'We can hold another one later, when the picture will be more complete. A partial reconstruction tomorrow could well give us an idea or two.'

'Very well.' This was going to mean long and hard work far into the night.

The doors swung open and in came three people concerned with the evening's opera, Monsieur Maurice Blanc, the artistic director, Monsieur Rochebrun, the musical director, and Lakmé herself, swathed in furs and carrying a huge bouquet. There was a spatter of handclapping from those opera-goers already seated. Ernestine gave a gleaming smile and a wave to everyone, and tossed a red rose from the bouquet to an elderly gentleman who looked rich. As her eyes swept round the room she gave a delighted little scream, thrust her bouquet into the arms of Monsieur Rochebrun and ran across to Picard, throwing her arms round him and kissing him ecstatically.

'Chanteloup! My own darling Chanteloup!'

'Ernestine! My love! What a surprise!'

42

'Were you in front? Don't say you were in front and didn't come round to see me afterwards.'

'I didn't even know you were in the town, my adored one.'

'I'm not surprised; they don't go in for publicity in this place.'

'What were you singing?'

'Lakmé.'

'Did you manage the key-change in the last act?'

'Do I ever? No, I made a balls of it.'

The head waiter had seated her two companions at a table in the corner. She turned round and gave them a wave.

'You must come and join us,' she said to Picard. 'The conductor's a silly old fart, but the director's rather nice. Come along, I insist – and your friend as well.' For the first time she turned her eyes to Bonpain, who was now bright pink.

'Let me present Commissaire Bonpain,' said Picard.

'I know him. I know him already. He's a lamb.' Ernestine took them both by the hand and led them across the room, calling to the head waiter to place two more chairs at the table in the corner.

There was no need to present Bonpain to Messieurs Blanc and Rochebrun, both of whom greeted his arrival with restrained enthusiasm. Picard was introduced merely as a friend from Paris.

'A friend of my brother-in-law,' said Bonpain, keeping up the cover story.

'You gave me a very worrying afternoon yesterday, Commissaire,' said Monsieur Blanc.

'All over and done with,' said Bonpain, hoping that the subject wasn't going to be developed.

'And you were very uncooperative on the telephone.'

'You know how it is when you're busy.'

'I suppose I wasn't busy!' said Monsieur Blanc.

'For the second performance, let's get that key-change right,' said Monsieur Rochebrun to Ernestine.

'Sod the key-change,' said Ernestine. 'Let's have some lobster and champagne.'

Wednesday, 10 September

Ernestine and Picard lay side by side in bed in her room at the Hotel of the Loire and of the Golden Chariot. They were panting happily.

'You were always good at that, Chanteloup,' she said. 'I don't know why we ever broke up.'

'Because I was frequently out of Paris, and whenever I came back I used to find that you'd run off with somebody else.'

'But very seldom for long, and not just with any old body else, darling – I mean, the last one was a minister.'

'Are you still with him?'

'Sort of.'

'I shall be very surprised if he survives the next Cabinet reshuffle.'

'So will he. I suppose you're working here.'

'Yes, and you're going to make it very difficult to concentrate.'

'Would it be anything to do with what I was mixed up in on Monday?'

'What were you mixed up in on Monday?'

'I'd been having a quiet swim, and I was just putting my clothes on, and then everybody started carrying on, and apparently some poor little man had been murdered, and there was a sweet policeman, who adores opera and is a great fan of mine, who put handcuffs on me.'

'Nothing you say can surprise me, darling.'

'Will you move to this hotel tomorrow?'

'No.'

'Why not? It's much better than that stuffy old Grand Hotel of the Baths and of Serbia.'

'The job I'm doing makes it better for me to be there. Incidentally, I hope I can rely on you to keep my identity a secret.'

'Of course, darling. Shall we try the same again?'

44

'Let it be tomorrow, *Monsieur le Commissaire,*' the man from Paris had said, and Bonpain had accepted the challenge. The commissariat had been working at full pressure most of the night, arranging a preliminary reconstruction of the crime. A large plan of the bathing establishment had been drawn and, where such information had been elicited, the names or descriptions of the occupants had been written in the squares representing the twelve cabins for females on the seaward side and the twelve for males on the landward side. The cabins, together with all other equipment, had been carefully put together again at first light. On the promenade were hand-written notices, reading: 'Were you bathing on Monday morning? If so, you may be able to help the police solve a dastardly crime. Please report at Madame Berthier's bathing establishment.' Inspector Lautier was sitting in the pay booth, ready to take testimonies, few of which were expected to be of the slightest value, but it was, to put it at the least, a pleasant late-season excitement for the holidaymakers. The newspapers, of course, were full of the murder, and several of them printed censorious articles about the scandalous mixing of the sexes at sea-bathing establishments. All in all, it was the best possible publicity for a town which had a growing reputation for clean fun and fresh air.

Verdi had been collected as he left the opera house, tearstained from the emotional experience of Ernestine's Lakmé, and put in charge of the making-out and delivery of convocation forms, the first of which, in the gasworks area, he delivered as early as six o'clock. It was due to his consideration and admiration that Ernestine was the last to receive hers, at nine o'clock.

It was an authoritative knock at the door. Ernestine opened her eyes and looked at the clock on her bedside table. In an angry voice, she called out, 'I gave no instructions for a call this morning; I don't want to be disturbed.'

A voice as authoritative as the knock said, 'Police, Madame.'

Ernestine shook Picard, who opened sleepy eyes. She put her finger to her lips and murmured: 'It's the police, darling. Better get under the bedclothes.'

She jumped out of bed, her naked body glowing in the sunlight which shone through the pink curtains. 'Just a minute,' she called. She scurried round the room, collecting Picard's neatly-folded clothes and his hat and his shoes and umbrella, and pushed them under the bedclothes beside him. Then she piled pillows on top of him, whispered, 'Stop breathing, darling,' slipped on a transparent peignoir and sat down on the edge of the bed, hiding him as much as she could. 'Enter,' she called.

It was Verdi, adoration in his eyes.

'You are a goddess,' he said.

'Thank you, M'sieur.'

'I was in the front row of the second gallery. You were magnificent.'

'It's a little early in the morning for such heady compliments.'

'How Delibes would have loved to hear you! Never has the "Bell Song" been sung so exquisitely.'

'I'm delighted to hear you thought so.'

'During the last act, I was sobbing. Such dignity! Although you loved him, you still kept him at arm's length.'

'You were present, I think, when I told the commissaire the tenor has bad breath. I appreciate the kind things you say, M'sieur, but I wish to go back to sleep.'

' "Beautiful lady with all the virtues, never was woman more fair".'

'You exaggerate.'

'Nabucco. Act II. The duet.'

'Ah yes, I've sung it.'

'I've brought these for you.' From behind his back he produced a bouquet. Nestling among the blooms was a document in an official envelope. He stepped forward to lay it on the bed. To stop him coming too far, she moved towards him, putting out her hands for the flowers. The peignoir opened and her left breast fell out. Verdi gazed at it with rapture.

'I'll read your note presently,' she said, putting back the breast.

'It isn't a note, Madame. It's a convocation.'

'For me?'

'There's to be a reconstruction of the crime at three o'clock.'

'I have nothing to reconstruct.'

'You have to do just what you were doing yesterday morning at the time of the murder.'

'You're getting me down on the beach just to stand in my drawers in a bathing cabin?'

Verdi blushed and cast down his eyes. 'Until this afternoon, Madame.' He went.

'It's just occurred to me,' said Picard, sitting up and looking for

46

his undervest in the tangle of clothes which surrounded him, 'that last night I told a young man in my department to wait in my room for my return. He should be hungry by now.'

'What's this reconstruction caper?'

'I ordered it, my love.'

'If it's your show, then you can give me a note excusing me from taking part. I've a rehearsal this afternoon.'

'Of what?'

'*Madame Butterfly.*'

'You've sung that so often you could do it in your sleep.'

'Not the way they put it on here.'

'Besides, I want you on the beach with me. I want you by my side wherever I am, darling Ernestine.'

'Bollocks,' said Ernestine, affectionately.

Inspector Vaquin was visiting the last two or three suspects on a long list he had compiled of ladies who were rumoured to oblige gentlemen. These borderline, unsubstantiated cases needed a subtle approach. He entered a baker's shop in the Rue Jules-Ferry. A middle-aged blonde of generous build greeted him with a wide smile.

'M'sieur.'

'Madame.' He raised his hat.

'What can I do for M'sieur?'

'What is the speciality here?' he asked, provocatively.

'How do you feel about a nice warm loaf?'

'What else?' he asked, angling for further revelation of what he suspected might well be a code.

'Something soft and sweet? Perhaps a couple of firm, milky brioches? Or a rum baba?'

The language was evocative, but he wasn't sure yet. If it was a code, it was a painfully unoriginal one. 'They sound enticing,' he said. 'Are they very expensive?'

'That depends.'

'On what?'

'On what you call expensive.'

'Are you on your own, or have you some friends here?'

'There are two other young ladies in the back room.'

'What are they doing?'

'Nothing at the moment. Do you fancy a roll with chocolate?

It seemed conclusive enough, although he knew of no black talent in town other than Miss Barbara at Madame Zizi's. He blew his whistle, and two of his men ran in from the van which was parked outside. He led the way through the bead curtains into the back room of the shop. Two girls were sitting on a settee. They were wearing homely dresses which covered them from neck to ankle and they were receiving religious instruction from the *curé*, Father Gérard, who, through his habitual haze of alcohol, was running through the beatitudes.

'Sorry, Father,' said Vaquin. 'Some wrong information.'

'You are doing God's work, my son,' hiccoughed the *curé*.

Bonpain was on the telephone to the Sureté, in Paris.

'Are you there?'

'Yes, *Monsieur le Commissaire*.'

'Who am I speaking to?'

'My name is Maigret, Jules*. I'm a new man.'

'I have a matter here to be treated with great discretion. It concerns a young woman – an opera singer – named Ernestine Masson, known as Thibault. She lives at 197, Avenue du Bois-de-Boulogne. I want to know if she's the mistress of the Minister of Justice.'

'You want me to ask her?'

'Certainly not. Anyway, she's here.'

'So you can ask her.'

'I can do no such thing.'

'I see, you want me to ask him.'

'There are other ways of finding out something than by asking the person concerned. If you wish to do well in the police, you should remember that. Call me back.' He replaced the receiver.

Grunwald was hungry and bored. He had read the whole of the Colette Willy novel, and was now reduced to playing noughts-and-crosses with himself on the lining paper in the drawers. He was delighted to see Picard return.

'Well, now,' he said, noticing the crumpled state of Picard's attire, 'it looks as if you've had quite a night.'

'Some very intensive work one way and another,' confirmed Picard,

---

* It appears likely that this young man afterwards became the celebrated Commissaire Maigret. In *La Première Enquête de Maigret* (Presses de la Cité, Paris, 1949) Georges Simenon reveals that Maigret joined the Sureté in 1913.

'including considerable physical activity.' He justified the latter statement to himself by the fact that he had hit the doctor.

'Have you breakfasted?' asked Grunwald.

'I've had a cup of coffee.' Indeed he had, basking in the sunshine outside a café on the promenade.

'Do you mind if I go and get some?'

'Very well, but don't be long. We have a busy day ahead of us. There's a reconstruction of the crime this afternoon.'

The breakfastless Grunwald left the room.

After changing his clothes and giving the valet instructions to sponge and press the suit he had just taken off, Picard strolled upstairs and knocked on the door of 226/7/8, the corner suite on the second floor.

'Come in,' called an English voice. In a white suit, with a red rose in his buttonhole, Colonel Withers was at the dressing-table, waxing the ends of his moustache.

'Well, where is it?'

'Where is what, Colonel?'

'The glass of apricot juice I ordered.'

'I'm not a member of the hotel staff, Colonel Withers.'

'Who are you then? Don't just stand there like a dismounted civilian.'

'I'm Grunwald's superior.'

'Almost anybody is superior to Grunwald.' Withers laughed at his own joke.

'I suppose His Majesty hasn't returned.'

'His Majesty will return when His Majesty is good and ready to return. The trouble with you people is that you've never been out on a party. Just because His Majesty isn't back at teatime, Grunwald goes off his feed like a gundog with croup. Now he's dragged you into it, whoever you are –'

'Chanteloup Picard.' He bowed.

'Is that so? Damn it, if it's a good party, there's no reason why he shouldn't be adrift for three days.'

'I don't want to take up your time, Colonel . . .'

'Believe me, my dear fellow, you won't. I've got a little deal on with a blue-eyed filly and I'm off in a few minutes. Ah!'

A waiter arrived with a glass of apricot juice, which Withers took eagerly. 'Believe it or not,' he said, 'I used to drink a lot of alcohol.' The little red veins weaving and bursting all over his face, together with a pair of poached-egg eyes with tomato-red rims, made the fact perfectly credible. 'Then I found it was affecting my performance – if you see what I mean. Well, I said to myself, you can't have every-thing – it's one thing or another – so now I subsist mainly on shell-fish and fruit juice; I think they both do you a lot of good in that direction. What are you here for?'

'It's the job of my department to provide protection.'

'His Majesty and I are two grown men with considerable experi-ence of the world, and we don't need any nosey minders following us about.'

'Colonel, we work as discreetly and unobtrusively as possible, and it's in order not to trouble His Majesty that I come to you, one of his oldest friends and comrades-in-arms.'

'Comrades-in-arms? He was never a cavalryman – and besides, we were in different armies.'

'I was referring to the Harrow OTC.'

'Oh, that. He was never more than a bloody lance-corporal.'

'We know that you are as concerned as any of his most loyal subjects that no harm should come to him.'

'He never learned to roll his puttees properly,' said the colonel, pursuing his own train of thought.

'Even in a holiday town like this, a head of state is vulnerable.'

'If anyone started anything, he and I would see him off.'

'I'm sure of it, and I'm also sure he confides in you about every-thing.'

'He's never kept a secret from me in his life: not even at Harrow during that unfortunate business about the tobacconist's daughter – but that's nothing to do with you.'

'To the best of your knowledge, Colonel, has His Majesty any enemies? Can you think of anyone who would wish to harm him?'

Withers pondered for a moment. 'Socialists,' he said at last. 'Anarchists too, of course.'

'I can assure you that every known or suspected anarchist or socialist is watched the whole time. Have you any particular one or ones in mind?'

'All of 'em, I should think. I'd put 'em up against a wall, if I had my way.'

'Anybody else?'

'That tobacconist, I dare say – but I doubt if he's still alive now.'

Picard bowed and withdrew. From his balcony, he watched the

colonel leave the hotel. He then ran upstairs again and let himself into suite 226/7/8 with a special key. He searched the rooms thoroughly. Apart from the return half of a first-class ticket from Mittenstein-Hoffnung, His Majesty did not appear to possess a single scrap of paper, and if one excluded a small collection of pictorial cuttings from *La Vie Parisienne* the same could be said about the colonel.

Inspector Vaquin had no progress to report. Despite the most detailed questioning of all the women on his list, he had been unable to pick up any information about the deceased middle-aged man with a round face and small moustache.

Now that the identity of the murdered man had been established, Bonpain knew that little of use was likely to emerge from the Morals Squad's efforts, but it did no harm to have the bottom of the pool stirred up occasionally, for one never knew what might float to the surface.

'I shall need your help this afternoon at the reconstruction of the crime, Vaquin. We shall inevitably have a large crowd on the promenade, watching the proceedings, so we'll have your men among them on villain-watch.'

'Very good, *Monsieur le Commissaire*.' Vaquin sniffed. So his highly-trained squad of specialists was to spend the afternoon looking for pickpockets!

Lautier entered. 'The mayor is here, *Monsieur le Commissaire*.'

'Zut!' said Bonpain. 'Show him in, Lautier; let's get it over. No, stay where you are, Vaquin,' he added as the inspector politely made for the door. 'What can I do for you, *Monsieur le Maire?*' he asked the plump ironmonger who was puffing his way in. 'I'm afraid I'm under great pressure of work this morning.'

'I'm sure you are, *Monsieur le Commissaire*, and I know I speak for every citizen when I express the hope that your efforts will speedily be crowned with success. A murder in our fair town!' He shook his head until his dewlaps flapped.

'No one can regret it more than we do, and I can assure you that it was in no way due to a lack of vigilance on our part,' said Bonpain.

'But possibly to a lowering of the moral standards to which we have been accustomed.'

'If you'd care to explain yourself...'

'I refer to the new variety of adjoining cabins installed at Madame Berthier's establishment. They offer obvious temptations which were

51

avoided in the separate bathing machines which could be drawn down to the water's edge.'

'As you are fully aware, *Monsieur le Maire*, this is a progressive watering place to which we wish to attract the more sophisticated type of visitor, those who are wealthy and well-travelled, members of international society . . .' He was tempted to add 'even royalty', but thought better of it. 'We should not be confined by out-dated bourgeois conventions, dear though they may be to some of us. We have to consider the new and livelier influences of the arts, such as the novels of Colette Willy, the cinematographic comedies of Max Linder . . .'

'I speak for popular morality, *Monsieur le Commissaire*; I speak against what offends my own moral sense and that of my dear wife – and I may have to make my views known in more influential quarters.'

He turned towards the door, but Inspector Vaquin stepped in his way. 'I saw a friend of yours last night, *Monsieur le Maire*,' he said. 'I looked in at Cousin Emile's, and young Suzy was there. You'd never think she was only thirteen, would you? And I shouldn't go there on Tuesday evening, if I were you, because we're going to run the place into the ground.'

The mayor went even whiter than usual, swallowed hard, dribbled a little at the corners of his mouth, and scuttled out of the door.

Vaquin looked rather shame-facedly at Bonpain. 'I'm sorry,' he said, 'I just couldn't help it. I love sinners, but I hate hypocrites.'

'I'm most grateful to you, Vaquin; it should keep him quiet for quite a time. I suppose we shall get a visit from *Monsieur le Curé* next.'

'I doubt it, *Monsieur le Commissaire*,' said Vaquin, glancing up at the clock. 'He'll be well pissed by now.'

By a quarter to three, there was a large crowd on the promenade by the bathing establishment. There were several unauthorized stalls selling *crêpes*; Aristide Laperdrix had set up his *guignol* show for children, although in forty years he had never before moved it from his pitch opposite the Opera House; there were at least five newspaper sellers, and the big event of the afternoon was an aeroplane which swooped overhead with a press photographer leaning out of it. Inspector Vaquin and his men made up for a poor morning by arresting a shoplifter and two deserters.

The bathing establishment, although closed for business, was also crowded because, in addition to the police and those with convocations, there were numerous other people with various unlikely excuses for attending this exciting event. It was nearly four o'clock before matters were reasonably under control. Picard, with Grunwald at his side, was seated at an upstairs window of the commissariat, watching the proceedings through binoculars. So far, it had been possible to trace only five of those who had occupied cabins two mornings before. These included Ernestine, but excluded His late Majesty.

'It's all a waste of time,' muttered Bonpain to himself.

'By insisting on this, I made them do as much work last night as they'd have done in three days,' said Picard to Grunwald.

As accurately as could be arranged, everyone had taken up the position he or she occupied at the time of the murder. Bonpain had ordered the slovenly Gibeau to represent the victim, because he was roughly of the same stature; he was dressed in the dead man's clothes and had a false moustache gummed to his upper lip.

The commissaire had Peyronnet show Gibeau to a cabin on the landward or male side, and he then timed with a chronometer the number of seconds it took Gibeau, once Peyronnet's back was turned, to climb the dividing fence and reach the cabin on the seaward side in which the king had met his doom.

Bonpain made them run through the scene four or five times, each time to greater appreciation and applause from the crowd, but then he couldn't think what to do next, so he went by himself into the king's cabin. Like all the others, it was of white-painted matchboarding, with two pegs on each side wall and a fixed wooden bench at the rear. Light came from a glass panel in the roof, and there was a small, round looking-glass screwed to the inside of the door. On the floor was a section of the same duckboarding which formed the paths between the two rows of cabins. Next door, Ernestine was trilling a few roulades and cadenzas.

In each of the side walls, about seventy centimetres from the floor, was a roughly made hole. Removing his hat, Bonpain dropped to one knee and peered through the hole into the empty cabin; he found that his field of vision encompassed most of the area from the edge of the bench to the door, up to about shoulder height. He rose to his feet, turned, and then knelt to the hole on the side of Ernestine's cabin.

Whether because it was a warmish day, or because her theatrical training had conditioned her to play every scene to its full, or just to ridicule the whole business, she had removed her dress and petticoats and was standing, facing the door, in her bodice and drawers, doubtless watching herself in the looking-glass as she performed her vocal exercises. The drawers were of a delicate oyster-shell silk, neatly ruched at the waist where they were secured by an inlet elastic. Cut to a biform pattern with an inserted gusset, they fitted tightly to the curve of the buttocks and encased the thighs quite firmly down to just above the knees, where they flared slightly and were lengthened by the addition of a two-centimetre band of valenciennes lace, gathered slightly and hand-sewn at eight stitches to the centimetre. Nestling below the lace were two garters of matching satin decorated with a single row of hand-embroidered pink roses each about forty millimetres in diameter.

Bonpain had no time to notice more than these basic details before the agreeable spectacle was replaced by a very close view of a clear grey eye which looked into his. The vocal exercises were replaced by a gurgling laugh of delighted amusement.

'Peek-a-boo, *Monsieur le Commissaire*,' said Ernestine. Bonpain rose hastily to his feet, scarlet with embarrassment. He pulled open the door and stepped out, almost bumping into Picard.

'Good afternoon, *Monsieur le Commissaire*.' Bonpain quailed under the polite smile of the younger man. Did he suspect his recent activity? Had he realized the cause of Ernestine's merry laugh? Would Ernestine later recount the incident to Picard? Would she retail it all round the town?

He stammered as he returned Picard's greeting.

'Come back with me into that cabin,' said Picard, pushing open the door which Bonpain had just shut behind him.

Bonpain did as he was asked. Ernestine was practising the tricky key-change in the last act which had not satisfied her the evening before.

'Ernestine,' called Picard.

'Is that you, Chanteloup?'

'It is. Will you be a darling and shut up?'

'It's terribly boring in here, with nothing to do.'

'Then open the door and watch what's going on.'

'I can't. I'm not decent.'

'Then make yourself decent,' said Picard.

'I thought the idea was for everyone to be just the way we were two mornings ago.'

'I didn't order a performance, just a preliminary reconstruction.'

The thought struck Bonpain that he had taken a serious physical risk. Suppose Ernestine had used another sharp instrument! He shivered.

'It was a mistake, *Monsieur le Commissaire*,' said Picard, 'to have had these cabins taken apart.'

'I was searching for the murder weapon.'

'And destroying whatever other evidence there was to be found.'

'What evidence could there be? The huts were in constant use, so the chance of finding useful fingerprints was negligible.'

'There were bloodstains.'

'Which were photographed.'

'I've seen the photographs; they are hardly to be compared with the real thing.' Picard took a magnifying glass from his pocket and examined a faint, brown smear on the wall which was common to that cabin and to Ernestine's. 'You see how little definition is left after your men have been pulling the place to pieces. Now – ' He picked his way past Bonpain, carefully brushed the bench with the back of his hand, and sat down with the commissaire, tight-lipped, standing and facing him like a schoolboy summoned before a master. 'Let us recapitulate. In the cabin on your left is, and was, Madame Masson, professionally known as Mademoiselle Ernestine Thibault. She was in the process of dressing herself ...'

'Just what I'm doing now, darling,' came Ernestine's voice.

'And it is indeed possible that the process had been, or was being, observed by the gentleman in this cabin,' continued Picard.

'The gentleman whose identity we do not yet know,' interjected Bonpain, slowly and carefully, for Ernestine's benefit.

'Exactly,' said Picard.

'He was welcome, whoever he was,' said Ernestine. 'It didn't cost me anything.'

'You're a shameless woman,' called Picard, 'and if you interrupt again I'll have you arrested for the second time.'

'You wouldn't dare,' said Ernestine, cheerfully. 'If I told everything I know about you – '

'That's called blackmail, and I have a witness. Have you got your clothes on yet?'

'Why don't you have a look through the little hole, and see.'

55

'It wouldn't amuse me, darling. Why don't you go for a stroll?'

'I shall go down to the theatre; I'm supposed to be rehearsing *Madame Butterfly*.'

'Do that, and then come back here and I'll buy you a drink before dinner.'

'You can buy me dinner as well,' said Ernestine. The door of the adjoining cabin opened and shut, and her shoes click-clacked down the duckboards.

'Do you still think she did it?' asked Picard.

'The evidence would seem to say so.'

'And the evidence is?'

'First, she's a beautiful woman.'

'And therefore a temptation for surreptitious observation?'

Bonpain blushed for the third time. 'To those given to that sort of thing.'

'We don't yet know who was in the adjoining cabin on the other side of us.'

'The bloodstain is on the wall common to the cabin she occupied, and not on the other.'

Picard scratched his chin, evoking the scene slowly. 'The man was killed by a sharp instrument being driven through the thin bone at the side of the nose and penetrating the brain. It is the kind of wound which produces instant bleeding and intense pain, and the man's instinct would have been to press his hand to his face and stagger out for help. He was getting to his feet, one eye would have been covered by his hand, he was in a state of shock, and he was groping for the latch on the door, and the latch, you will notice, is on the side of Mademoiselle Thibault's cabin. He'd have made a bloodstain on that wall irrespective of which hole he had been looking through. I submit that it is just as likely that he had been observing whoever was in the other cabin, and therefore just as likely that he was stabbed from that side.'

'I have to admit the possibility.'

'Also, as you will have gathered, Mademoiselle Thibault happens to be a personal friend of mine.'

'I had indeed gathered that.' There was a hint of a sneer in Bonpain's voice. There was always the chance that it was Picard's turn to feel embarrassment, although he displayed no trace of it.

'Let me assure you, Commissaire, that the friendship would count for nothing if for a single moment I suspected her to be guilty.'

'I hardly need that assurance.' So there was indeed some embarrassment behind that smooth mask. Good!

'And I know that despite her forthcoming manner she is a very sensitive young lady. I am told that her performance last night was almost flawless: I can't believe that would have been the case with a recent murder on her conscience. So – who was in the other cabin?'

'I've spent hours trying to get that information from Madame Berthier and from Peyronnet. Neither can remember.'

'Nor can they remember who was in the cabin beyond it?'

'No.'

'They must be encouraged. They must be interrogated again.'

'I'll send for them.'

'Let's find some more convenient place to work in.'

'The commissariat?'

'Which, for Madame Berthier and Peyronnet has all the associations of forgetfulness. Let's try somewhere else.'

They left the cabin and turned right towards the pay booth and the entrance. This was the only way out, because a wall of stretched canvas blocked the other end, ensuring privacy for the users of the establishment and ruling out the possibility of anyone getting in for nothing.

'How about the restaurant, Le Florida?' asked Picard.

'The food is lamentable.'

'But we're not going to eat, my dear colleague. They can give us a table and serve us an aperitif.' At the word 'aperitif' Bonpain brightened.

Inspector Verdi was demonstrating to a knot of his fellow inspectors how he had found the murdered man lying on the duckboards, and was telling them of the resourceful manner in which he had handled the situation. To add dramatic verisimilitude, he had persuaded Gibeau to lie down in the position in which the man had been found. 'I knew at once that it was a case of murder,' Verdi was saying.

'And an opportunity to put handcuffs on a pretty woman,' jeered a sceptical Inspector Hanoteau.

The men touched their hats as Bonpain and Picard passed, Inspector Gibeau sitting up to do so. In the pay booth, Inspector Lautier was dealing with the last of those who had queued to volunteer information. Bonpain raised an eyebrow to enquire whether anything of significance had come to light, but Lautier shook his head.

'We're going to Le Florida,' said Bonpain, reaching for the plan of the cabins, which had been placed in Lautier's care, and tucking it under his arm. 'Send us Madame Berthier and Peyronnet, one at a time.'

In the cool of the empty restaurant, they mopped their foreheads and ordered drinks from a petite dark-haired waitress named Anne-Marie.

After they had dealt with Madame Berthier, further drinks were necessary, because she had been tiresome and querulous, complaining about her lack of sleep the previous night, the loss of trade due to her having repeatedly to close her establishment, the lack of civility on the part of the personnel of the commissariat, the low rates of pay at the water-works which made it necessary for her to contribute to the family exchequer, the high rate of taxation, the pains in her poor feet, and the fact that the fine weather couldn't last for ever. She could add nothing to her previous statements about the case, and she swept out with an admonition that they should make sure that Peyronnet locked up at the end of the day.

In his turn, Peyronnet was also difficult, saying that he had already remembered all he could, and was in no mood to go through it all again. Bonpain was debating with himself whether he could bear to take him out drinking, in the hope that a dozen or so aperitifs would enliven his memory, when Lautier appeared in the doorway, showing signs of excitement. Bonpain got up and went to meet him.

'There's a Dutch lady outside, *Monsieur le Commissaire*. She has some interesting things to say.'

'What about?'

'About Peyronnet, and about the occupants of two of the cabins.'

'Bring her in,' said Bonpain.

Madame Apelbommel was a stiff, fierce little woman, who sat bolt upright in her chair, scowling at Peyronnet.

'Madame, will you have the goodness to repeat to us what you were telling the inspector outside?' asked Bonpain.

She required no further urging. In a thick, puddingy accent, she revealed facts that made Peyronnet go purple and shuffle his feet. To start with, she thought it quite disgraceful that ladies and gentlemen should share the same bathing establishment, separated only by a trellis fence, and with cabins which shared matchboard walls with adjoining cabins. She couldn't imagine such an arrangement in Holland, where she had been warned of the reprehensible attitude of the French to such matters. Slowly, she worked her way to the point. On Monday morning, she had been for a swim and had been allotted cabin number 11 on the ladies' side. To her horror, while dressing, she heard sounds of laughter and improper carrying-on between a male and female in the adjoining cabin on her left.

'Cabin number 12,' said Bonpain, consulting his chart. 'The end one.'

'How did you know the carrying-on was improper?' asked Picard.

Madame Apelbommel revealed that, unable to believe the testimony of her ears, she had confirmed the matter by peering briefly through the hole which was standard equipment in the walls of all the cabins. She refused to soil her lips by describing in detail what she had seen, but it was improper all right, oh *ja*!

'A lot of lies,' said Peyronnet. 'There's never any question of two people of opposite sexes sharing a cabin when I'm on duty.'

'Madame,' said Bonpain, 'Didn't it occur to you to complain to the management on your way out?'

'It certainly did, but when I was ready to depart I saw there was a gentleman lying on the ground, apparently the victim of an accident or a seizure, and as I have a horror of such incidents I hurried off. I had no idea that it was the result of a dastardly crime,' she added, quoting from the poster on the promenade.

'Could you describe the two persons in the adjoining cabin?' asked Picard.

'There's no need, they're both here,' said the Dutch lady. 'It was him – ' and she pointed at Peyronnet, ' – and her' – and she pointed at Anne-Marie, who was behind the bar.

Peyronnet protested. Anne-Marie giggled.

'Furthermore,' continued Madame Apelbommel, 'as there was no one to show users of cabins to their rightful sides, there was a shameful mingling of sexes everywhere. Why, there was a man in the cabin on my right.'

'Cabin number 10,' said Bonpain, 'The one next to the dead man.'

'Did you have a look at him too?' asked Picard eagerly.

'There was no need. I had no complaints to make about him, except that he was on the wrong side, and I presume that was not his fault.'

'How did you know it was a man?' asked Bonpain.

'From the way he coughed, whistled and stamped about – and, at one point, he sang.'

'To himself?'

'Presumably.'

'What did he sing?'

' "The Soldiers' Chorus", from *Faust*.'

'In what kind of voice?' asked Picard.

'A young baritone.'

'Did he know the words?'

'He la-laed it.'

'Pity.'

The Dutch lady could provide no further information, so she was sent on her way, having given her address as the Hotel of the Casino and of Paris. Peyronnet was also dismissed, pleading that his improper carrying-on with Anne-Marie – whom he had admitted under the canvas wall, and not for the first time – should not be revealed to Madame Berthier.

'So we are making progress,' said Picard. 'It may be slow, but it is progress.'

Bonpain was staring at the chart of the cabins. 'Monsieur Picard – ' he said, with amazement in his voice.

'What is it, Commissaire?'

'If it wasn't Mademoiselle Thibault who killed the king, but the occupant of the other adjoining cabin, then it means that the king was looking through a hole at the young man who was singing.'

'Exactly.'

'So His Majesty must have been . . .' Bonpain paused.

Picard finished the sentence. '. . . a man of unorthodox interests.'

Bonpain thought things over for a moment. 'Obviously, the young man, having observed those unorthodox interests, was singing to let the king know that there was a young male in the adjoining cabin on the left.'

'Yes.'

'To entice him to look through the hole – so that he could stab him.'

'Of course.'

'So he sang "The Soldiers' Chorus" from *Faust*. That's hardly my idea of a siren song.'

'He's probably not your idea of a siren.'

'I was asked to give the king police protection,' said Bonpain, 'but I should have been told to warn my men to protect themselves.'

Bonpain and Grunwald were sitting in the bar of the Grand Hotel of the Baths and of Serbia. It was late and they had been sitting there some time. On the table in front of them was a sizeable pile of saucers, each of them marked 1F 25.

'You have to hand it to Picard,' said Grunwald. 'Having the reconstruction today was very useful.' To his surprise, he had not yet been sacked, so he was being on everybody's side in case he should be given another chance. 'Incidentally, I was most impressed by the likeness of your Inspector Gibeau to the late king. I had quite a shock when he first appeared.'

Bonpain accepted the compliment for himself, waving it aside as airily as Monsieur Lucien Guitry might if complimented on the excellence of his supporting company. 'I know my men,' he said.

The door from the front hall swung open and Colonel Withers strode in. On the shoulders of his faultless evening coat were traces of face-powder, and his white tie was lightly touched with rouge. He nodded firmly to the barman. No words were necessary and the man sprang immediately to pour out a large glass of apricot juice. Having taken a sustaining draught, Withers turned to survey the room, which was almost empty. He saw Grunwald and walked towards him. Grunwald rose and bowed. He presented Bonpain, who also rose and bowed. Colonel Withers, who had had a tiring evening, sat down heavily on the chair which Grunwald hurried to place for him.

'A gorgeous day,' said Bonpain.

'I've been indoors,' said Withers.

'I'm sure it's going to be fine tomorrow,' said Grunwald, keeping up his side of the conversation.

'Where's His Majesty?' asked Withers.

'I'd hoped you'd be able to tell me,' said Grunwald.

'Not my job,' said Withers. 'Yours.'

'You told my superior this morning that we weren't to worry if His Majesty was adrift as long as three days.'

'Who's worrying? I'm not worrying, I just want to know where he is.' He turned to Bonpain. 'Do you know?'

'No, *Monsieur le Colonel*.'

'He was fooling around with some of your chaps this afternoon.'

'My chaps?'

'I popped out for a breath of air this afternoon, and there was HM on the beach with a lot of policemen.'

'Ah, yes – quite possible, *Monsieur le Colonel*; there were a number of my men on the beach.' The fact that Inspector Gibeau's impersonation might be seen by Withers was something that had not occurred to him – nor, apparently, to Picard or Grunwald.

'They're very small, French policemen,' said Withers.

'You think so?'

Grunwald asked a leading question. 'Colonel, during your long friendship with His Majesty, have you noticed any – er – partiality to the company of policemen?'

'Partiality?'

'To policemen – or any other uniformed men. Sailors, for instance.'

'Mittenstein-Hoffnung hasn't a navy.'

'I don't necessarily mean when he's at home – but when he's travelling.'

'They haven't a coastline, you see.'

'You've never noticed him spending time with sailors?' persisted Grunwald.

'Quite pointless, having a navy without a sea,' persisted Withers. 'Are you a sailor?'

'No, Colonel.'

'You seem preoccupied with sailors. Were you one once?'

Grunwald sighed. 'It was my boyhood dream to be a sailor, but I am a Jew, and somehow Jews don't look right as sailors.'

'The hats are the wrong shape,' said the colonel, nodding firmly to the barman.

It had been an exciting evening for Edouard Tinville-Lacombe. Just as he was leaving the *mairie*, a military motorcyclist had arrived from Paris, bearing an envelope covered with such legends as 'Personal', 'For the Eyes of the Addressee Only', 'Top Secret' and 'Highly Confidential', and heavily sealed. Salivating with excitement, the fat mayor broke open the packet: was his worth officially recognized at last? And was this the way in which the bestowal of high honour was intimated? Was he to be given a Ministry? Or invited to form a government? God knew that he could make a better job of it than the idiots whose vapourings were reported in the press.

Alas, it was none of those things, although the contents surely showed how much his perspicacity and trustworthiness were valued in high places. It was a letter from an official, whose signature was illegible, at the Quai d'Orsay, and it required the mayor to provide a room in which a highly secret meeting could be held at midnight. The bearer of the letter was to be shown a suitable room, and then given the keys of the building. The mayor and his staff were to go home at the usual time.

The mayor looked at the motorcyclist, heavily muffled and standing rigidly to attention before him. 'Er – do you think this room would be suitable?' he asked, waving a hand round his parlour.

His military visitor looked round, and nodded.

'Is there anything you wish to be supplied?'

The soldier shook his head.

'And my presence is not required?' The question had a wistful tone.

The soldier shook his head, more emphatically.

'Very well. I do hope you'll lock up after you.'

At ten minutes before midnight, the mayor stole into the dark doorway of the church of St Evian of the Running Sores, which faced the *mairie*. If, after all, his advice were needed, he would be right on the spot, and ready to earn his ribbon of the Legion of Honour.

'You won't be needed, *Monsieur le Maire*,' said a voice from the darkness beside him. 'I should go home and get a good night's sleep.' He turned and saw the tall figure of the soldier who had delivered the letter. Mumbling something about always taking a stroll before bed-time, Tinville-Lacombe disconsolately made for home. Honours would have to come to him by the slow grind, and not by the golden opportunity.

As he departed, he saw a light-coloured Daimler swing round the square and stop in front of the *mairie*. A top-hatted figure, carrying a heavy briefcase, alighted and was admitted to the building by the soldier.

A few seconds later, one of the taxis with a fringed white canopy, from outside the Grand Hotel of the Baths and of Serbia, stopped in its turn, and the trim figure of Chanteloup Picard stepped out. He, too, carried a heavy briefcase. Midnight struck.

63

Thursday, 11 September

In the mayor's parlour, the two men faced each other. The new arrival in the town was Charles Lavigny, Chanteloup Picard's chief.

'We're going to have a lot of talking to do, Picard. Have you everything necessary?'

Picard opened his briefcase. 'Two bottles of Latour '03. Monsieur Lavigny.'

'Excellent. I have some Tour d'Argent '94. I hope it hasn't been shaken too much.'

They filled two crystal glasses brought from the Quai d'Orsay and settled themselves on opposite sides of the mayoral desk, each with his heels on the blotter.

'What we have to do, Picard, is to stop a war.'

'As serious as that?'

'No kingdom likes losing its monarch, and a ridiculous little country like Mittenstein-Hoffnung hasn't got much else. I'm not going to say that if it were discovered that a Frenchman had done the deed then they'd declare war on us, but if the killer was a national of one of the neighbouring states – like Krasnia, for instance – then the army would be across the border in a matter of minutes.'

'So, whatever happens, we mustn't put the blame on a Krasnian.'

'I'm not even sure we put the blame on anyone.'

'Somebody killed him, and it's my job to find out who.'

'It would have been so much simpler if he had been assassinated in his own country.'

'But he wasn't.'

'Perhaps it could be made to look as if he was.'

'Difficult.'

'But possible. How cold is it in that cellar under the fish market?'

'Cold enough to preserve a body for a few days, if that's what you're getting at.'

'What are the local industries?'

'That apple liqueur?'

'That's no good.'

'Tomatoes?'

'Messy.'

'Salted cod?'

'That's better. Let's assume that a load of it is shipped to Mittenstein-Hoffnung by rail. It shouldn't be difficult to salt away a body in salted cod.'

'I see what you mean,' said Picard. 'Our agent would retrieve him at the other end, and arrange for him to be murdered all over again.'

'Exactly. How many people know that he's dead?'

'Apart from ourselves and one or two top men in Paris, the only ones to know the identity of the dead man are Commissaire Bonpain and Grunwald.'

'Plus the murderer.'

'Obviously.'

'How far have you got with that?'

Briefly, Picard described the events of the afternoon.

'The man's voice sang "The Soldiers' Chorus",' mused Lavigny, and quoted ' "Ready to fight or ready to die for our Native land". He doesn't sound like an anarchist.'

'He may have intended not to sound like an anarchist.'

'True.'

'Is there any competition for the throne? Is there a pretender?' asked Picard.

'If there is, it's the first time he's shown his hand – and a pretender doesn't kill and then keep quiet about it.'

'Is the succession assured?'

'The king has no children, but his brother has fourteen.'

'Does the brother succeed him?'

'Yes.'

'Willingly, do you think?'

'Probably not. He collects butterflies, and is writing the definitive book on the subject. Kingship would be an intolerable distraction.'

'How many people in Mittenstein-Hoffnung knew the king was coming here?' asked Picard.

'None so far as we know. When His Majesty went away on one

of his little jaunts, which he used to do once or twice a year, he would say that he was going to Baden-Baden for the waters. A hotel manager there used to cover for him, taking messages and forwarding any documents of importance.'

'Then the hotel manager knows that His Majesty was here.'

Lavigny looked at his watch. 'In about half an hour's time, the hotel manager will trip on the top step of his main staircase.'

'Fatally?'

'Indeed.'

'It seems drastic.'

'It is. When will you be able to despatch the load of salted cod?'

'By the afternoon or evening, and it should arrive the following day. It strikes me that we haven't sufficiently explored the homosexual angle.'

'There's no need. As soon as the body is off French soil, the investigation will be dropped.'

'A pity. Does that mean that someone of such eminence might be involved that he could not be pursued?'

'That would be an obvious conclusion for a cynical man such as yourself – but not so far as I know.'

'For my own satisfaction, I'd like to find the killer.'

'Unfortunately, we're not in this business for our own satisfaction.'

Picard took a sip of wine. He noticed with contentment that Lavigny's Tour d'Argent '94 was not a patch on his own Latour '03. 'By the time the body has reached Mittenstein-Hoffnung after three nights in the cellar of the fish market and a night in a trainload of salted cod, it won't be in the freshest of conditions.'

'Our agent will have to plant it in a situation which would justify its non-discovery for four or five days, and also account for the presence of fish scales.'

'Shouldn't the body be going to Baden-Baden, if that is where His Majesty is supposed to be?'

'Your suggestions seem to imply that nobody has devoted thought to this case. The first and most obvious consideration is that German pathology is considerably more advanced than is general in Mittenstein-Hoffnung; the German customs service is considerably more thorough than that on the Mittenstein-Hoffnung border; the countryside round Baden-Baden is much less conducive to the casual deposition of a body under fishy circumstances than the wilder terrain of Mittenstein-Hoffnung; our agent in Mittenstein-Hoffnung is much

66

more intelligent than our agent in Baden-Baden . . . shall I go on?'

'You've made your point.'

The mayor's parlour was warm and softly lit, and the chairs were comfortable. Picard had spent the early part of the evening in Ernestine's bed and his exertions had tired him. Fearful of dozing, he rose to his feet and walked over to one of the tall windows. The moon shone between fast-moving clouds. Down in the square, a newspaper was flapping round the base of a street lamp, and the branches of the plane trees were moving gently in the breeze.

On either side of the window projected the ornate carvings which covered the front of the building. Picard looked up, his eyes following the contours of a nude Goddess of Plenty. To his astonishment, he saw a man's boot planted on the lady's left breast, and above the boot there was the bottom of a trouser leg.

Even with his forehead pressed against the glass he could see no more so, with a quick gesture, he undid the catch and threw open the two casements of the window, projecting himself through on to a tiny balcony. After a glance to satisfy himself that the man above him was not the military motorcyclist, he grabbed the lower loop of a floral garland which screened the secret parts of Melpomene, and hoisted himself up. What was there about this town, he asked himself, that incited people to climb the outside of buildings? Only yesterday, Grunwald had ruined a good pair of trousers quite unnecessarily in scaling a drainpipe.

Seeing Picard disappear upwards, Lavigny in his turn came out on the balcony. 'Picard,' he called, 'where are you going?'

Picard did not answer because he needed his breath. The man he was pursuing had been able to place a foot on the left breast and elevate himself quite easily, but Picard found it the most slippery breast he had ever encountered, and he was now hanging desperately to an ear and a lock of hair.

'Picard, come down at once,' called Lavigny. 'This is most unmannerly. I was talking to you.'

Picard's quarry was climbing deftly among the spilled contents of a cornucopia which surmounted the second-floor windows. Picard risked some breath. 'Come down, whoever you are,' he shouted.

'Who are you shouting at, Picard?' asked Lavigny, because Picard's nearer bulk obscured his view of the higher climber.

'Lavigny, tell the soldier to go up on the roof,' called Picard.

'On the roof? Whatever for?'

'There's an intruder.'

'I can't see one. I think you're – woo!' Lavigny stopped in mid-sentence as a stone strawberry, cracked by many a frost and dislodged by one of the intruder's feet, hit him on the left temple. He retreated indoors, dabbing at himself with a silk handkerchief. Obviously there was something in what Picard had said, so he went to look for the soldier.

The intruder had climbed his way to above the third-floor windows and was now faced with a tricky overhang formed by a cornice below the roof. For a moment, he paused to take stock, while Picard was able to put on a turn of speed among the plentiful hand and foot-holds afforded by the cornucopia.

'Surrender yourself,' panted Picard. 'You can't escape. The roof is patrolled by soldiery.'

The reply was a laugh, and a few bars of 'The Soldiers' Chorus', la-laed in a pleasant, if breathless, baritone.

Picard blanched. It was foolhardy to climb the facade of any building in darkness; it was doubly foolhardy to do so in pursuit of an unknown intruder; it bordered on insanity to do so when that intruder was a murderer – and no ordinary murderer either, but a regicide!

Lavigny was stumbling down the dimly lit main staircase to the ground floor, calling as he went, 'Guard! Where are you?' The guard was not far away; he had discovered a large cupboard in one of the offices where there were facilities for making coffee, and he was just about to do so. Unfortunately, the gas-ring gave forth a loud and almost continuous popping sound and this, plus the fact that, being another musical man, he was launched into the second verse of Yvette Guilbert's 'Le Fiacre', made it impossible for him to hear Lavigny. In fact, it was not until Lavigny's hand grasped him by the sleeve that he realized he was needed. He snapped to attention.

'The roof!' shouted Lavigny. 'The roof!'

Confused, the soldier interpreted the words as a warning that the roof was about to descend, so he made for the front door, but Lavigny went after him, crying 'An intruder' and pulled him back to the stairs, pointing the way upwards. The soldier obediently led the way to the third floor, where they found themselves in a maze of store-rooms. Half a dozen were inspected before they found one which had a trapdoor in the ceiling, and then the soldier had to run down to the basement to find a step ladder.

Meanwhile, the intruder, having assessed the situation, had swung himself easily over the cornice and was sprawled in the lap of a seated figure of Scholarship, swinging his legs in space and watching Picard toil up after him. Picard's head for heights was not bad, but there are limits, and he was getting nauseous twinges of vertigo every time he glimpsed the ground. He stopped for a breather.

Lavigny and the soldier had mounted the step ladder and pushed up the trapdoor. They found themselves in a vast pitch-dark loft, smelling of mice and thick with old spiders' webs.

'Strike a match,' said Lavigny.

'I don't smoke,' replied the soldier.

Lavigny groped in his own pockets and found a box. The feeble flame of a single match revealed nothing. He struck a second and then passed the box to the soldier, who struck two more and passed it back again. By constantly passing the box back and forth, it was possible to keep four matches alight at a time, one in each of the four hands available. They did not need the matches to reveal that they were not on a solid floor but on wooden joists, and every time a foot slipped the plaster of the ceiling below was broken.

'There must be a door out on to the roof,' snapped Lavigny.

There was, but it was locked.

Picard had resumed his slow upward progress. Very kindly, the intruder was making signs, showing him where to plant his feet. It was helpful, but when he reached the overhang all Picard could do was groan and close his eyes. After a few moments, he risked a look down at the balcony from which he had started: it looked almost as far down as the ground, and very much smaller. 'Lavigny,' he shouted. 'Where are you, Lavigny?' There was no reply.

The intruder had risen to his feet and was standing arm-in-arm with a figure of Progress. Picard saw him taking something shiny from a canvas bag slung from his shoulder. A bomb?

'Who are you?' called Picard. 'What are you doing?'

There was a laugh, and another few bars of 'The Soldiers' Chorus'. Then the intruder gave a wave and disappeared from sight.

'You're not going to leave me!' cried Picard, whose vertigo was by this time really alarming. He did not even begin to tackle the cornice: he started cautiously to make his way down the cornucopia, clutching each strawberry and acorn as if it would be his last. He had just got a foot on the slippery left breast when Lavigny and the soldier appeared on the balcony.

'Haven't you caught him?' demanded Lavigny.

'I expect he's climbing down the back,' panted Picard. 'Go and get him.'

Lavigny and the soldier went back into the building and ran down the main stairs into a pall of thick black smoke.

'What the hell's all this smoke?' asked Lavigny, savagely.

The soldier groped his way into the office where he had been making coffee. He had not had time either to turn off the gas-ring or remove the saucepan. It was an old saucepan, mended with solder which had melted and set fire to the floor. The room was well alight.

'Telephone the fire brigade!' shouted Lavigny. He ran out of the front door and round to the back of the building. The intruder was sliding down the drainpipe and he was just a few feet from the ground.

'Ah!' said Lavigny, making a grab. The intruder swung lightly out of reach, then brought his right foot back in a swift kick that connected with Lavigny's stomach. 'Oh!' said Lavigny, collapsing on his backside.

The intruder dropped to earth, dusted his hands and strolled away. This time he was whistling.

Bonpain believed in mortifying the flesh as a penance for self-indulgence. He had sat far too long with Grunwald in the bar of the Grand Hotel of the Baths and of Serbia and, realizing that he was due for a hangover, had set the alarm clock to rouse him thirty minutes earlier than his usual early hour. It was a heavy grey morning, and his head throbbed in counter-rhythm to the click of his heels as he walked to the commissariat. Early though it was, Inspector Lautier was already at his desk, and rose respectfully to follow Bonpain into his office.

'Overnight report, please, Lautier,' said Bonpain, when the hand-shaking ceremony was over.

'Nothing concerning our major case, *Monsieur le Commissaire*.' He went on to recite from his notebook the minor incidents of drunkenness and beastliness which had relieved the tedium for the night staff.

'That all?'

'A small fire at the *mairie*. It was extinguished by the fire brigade.'

Bonpain grunted with satisfaction. He approved of any inconvenience, however minor, which smote the mayor.

Lautier hesitated a second before leaving the office. 'There was one rather curious occurrence, *Monsieur le Commissaire*.'

'Tell me.'

'It's not in itself a matter of illegality, I believe, although involving trespass and a lack of respect for our local institutions.'

'Get to the point, Lautier.'

'A number of our principal buildings have been – er – decorated.'

'Decorated? With what?'

'Chamber pots, Monsieur le Commissaire.'

'Which buildings?'

'The mairie, the Church of St Evian of the Running Sores, Madame Zizi's establishment and – er – this building.'

'How many chamber pots per building?'

'One – but invariably at the highest and least accessible point.'

'Is ours down?'

'Hanoteau shinned up and got it.'

'Good. And the others?'

'The fire brigade are at present occupying themselves with the task.'

'These objects were placed during the hours of darkness?'

'Evidently, and at a serious risk to life and property.'

'Some foolhardy youth, obviously.'

'Or youths, Monsieur le Commissaire. I suggest the matter is not worth spending any time on.'

'The fire brigade is spending some time on it – although they might as well be doing that as playing belote.'

Bonpain put through telephone calls to Picard and then Grunwald. He had staged what he considered a brilliantly successful reconstruction of the crime, and he had no intention of allowing himself to be relegated to the background by the two men from Paris now. He proposed to call a meeting in his office at which the next moves could be discussed. However, he found that both men had already left their hotel. What, he asked himself, could they be doing out so early?

His fears that he might no longer be at the forefront of the action were accentuated during the course of a telephone call from Edouard Tinville-Lacombe, who had arrived at the mairie to find a knot of juvenile spectators chuckling at the sight of a pink chamber pot crowning the head of the rooftop figure of Progress.

'The matter is being dealt with, Monsieur le Maire,' Bonpain said in an offhand manner. 'It must take its place below more important matters. I hear you had a fire.'

71

'A very minor one, I'm glad to say.'

'Nevertheless, our more important buildings must be protected. I'll have a word with the chief of the fire brigade, and ask him what additional precautions should be taken.' Bonpain was on good terms with the fire chief, and it would be easy and pleasant to have the mayor plagued with regulations involving the cluttering of the *mairie* with ladders, hoses, buckets of sand and draught-excluding doors. His headache felt better already.

'It's more important that the ridiculous object is taken from the roof.' The mayor was a boastful man and could not resist an opportunity to sound important, even at the expense of security, so he added, 'For your ears only, *Monsieur le Commissaire*, this building is being used for secret midnight meetings involving matters of national importance. In fact, only last night, some of the nation's leaders were here, protected by a detachment of troops.' The mayor hoped it would be wounding to the commissaire to hear that the military had been used rather than his own men.

Bonpain made an effort to sound neither wounded nor impressed. 'Was it the nation's leaders who set fire to the place?'

'It was an accident on the part of the soldiery.'

'You should have sent the soldiery up to get the chamber pot.' Bonpain hung up, and scratched his chin thoughtfully. If senior administrators had indeed been meeting at the *mairie* it could only have been in reference to the royal murder, and surely he should have been present. He slipped into a daydream. Suppose it were he who, by brilliant strokes of deduction and exceptional bravery, apprehended the killer. He imagined himself entering the mayor's parlour, a bloodstained bandage round his brow, presenting a handcuffed figure to the assembled leaders of the nation. 'I arrested him myself, messieurs. I thought it better not to confide in my men, so I went after him alone.' The nation's leaders rose, one by one, and grasped his hand. The President of the Republic had tears of gratitude in his eyes.

Grunwald had been roused at six o'clock by Picard, who had not been to bed. What with the conference at the *mairie*, the consumption both of a bottle of Latour '03 and of Tour d'Argent '94, the foolhardy attempt to pursue a presumed murderer up the front elevation of the building in darkness, and assisting in putting out a fire, the hours since midnight had been well filled, and it needed only the time it took to have a bath, a shave and a glass of fruit salts to bring him to daylight.

'I want you downstairs within twenty minutes,' he told the hungover Grunwald.

In fact, Grunwald was down in only nineteen minutes, but he looked so wan and bleary-eyed that it hardly appeared he would be of much use. 'Where are we going?' he asked.

'The railway station.'

'There are no trains before seven o'clock.'

'Freight trains run all night.'

Grunwald could see no point of mental contact with freight trains, but he asked no questions. They set off for the station. The taxi situation being what it was, they walked.

Picard led the way to the goods yard and demanded to see the freight superintendent. 'I have no doubt,' he said to that official, 'that you've had a great deal to do with shipping salted cod.'

The superintendent admitted that he had seen it done.

'What sort of wagon do you usually ship it in?'

The superintendent indicated a wagon marked 8 *Chevaux* – 40 *hommes*. It looked and smelled as if it had been occupied by both for a very long time.

'How much salted cod goes in one of those?'

'About twenty tonnes.'

Picard turned to Grunwald. 'How many kilos in a tonne?' Grunwald shook his head helplessly. Picard repeated the question to the superintendent. 'A thousand,' said the official, with a superior air.

'So that's twenty thousand kilos a wagon.'

'You could put it like that.'

'We'll deliver it within a few hours and load it at once. What time can it leave?'

'Depends where you want to send it.'

'Mittenstein-Hoffnung.'

The superintendent had scarcely heard of it. There was much opening of dusty timetables, freight registers and rule books. Picard turned to Grunwald again. 'Half full will be enough. Go and buy ten thousand kilos of salted cod. Telephone me when you've got it, and bring it here.'

'Where do I get it?' asked Grunwald.

'From a salted cod seller, I suppose. Use your intelligence.'

'How much is it?'

73

'Take several quotations and buy the cheapest.'

'Where do I get the money?'

'Ask for credit. The money will be forthcoming.' Picard returned his attention to the superintendent, who had been to fetch a colleague who brought another armful of timetables and a number of very tattered maps, which he began to spread on the floor.

Grunwald stumbled across the expanse of uneven cobbles which almost isolated the goods yard from the outer world. A narrow street cutting through an area of warehouses and stables led to the port, which seemed to be the right direction for his mission. A few yards along the street was a dark and depressing little café which possessed the single virtue of being open. It offered the prospects of alcohol and information, both of which he needed.

A naked gas-jet revealed that the room was densely occupied by citizens who breakfasted early on bitter black coffee and a fierce *eau-de-vie* which made Grunwald gasp. After two glasses, served to him by a short, thick man with a permanent dewdrop on the end of his large nose, he felt capable of beginning his day. He leaned across the zinc bar and consulted the dewdrop owner. 'Do you know a reliable cod salter?' he asked.

The matter was simpler than he had anticipated, because he was directed only two paces down the bar to a fat man in blue serge trousers and a rust-coloured smock.

'Monsieur,' said Grunwald. 'I wish to buy some salted cod.'

The fat man, who displayed a provident nature by keeping a half-smoked cigarette behind each ear, nodded and produced from a trousers pocket a small parcel wrapped in newspaper. 'I brought this for a friend who hasn't turned up,' he explained.

'I shall need more than that.'

'How much more?'

'Ten thousand kilos.'

On the strength of the amount, the fat man bought two large glasses of *eau-de-vie*. 'When do you want it?' he asked, after they had both taken a nourishing draught.

'Now.'

'Not a hope. There isn't that much in the town.'

'I'll pay well,' said Grunwald. He bought two more glasses.

The fat man summoned a small, bald friend with a cauliflower ear who summoned another friend who was young and flabby and had wet lips. There was a brief conference, and then the three of them

74

took Grunwald down the road to a vast shed. The smell of salted cod was overpowering. A bottle of *eau-de-vie* and four glasses were produced.

Against the wall leaned greenish-yellow slabs of what appeared to be decayed cardboard, each about two feet high. 'That's what you want,' said the fat man, indicating the nearest slab, against which a mongrel dog was urinating. 'You won't find better salted cod than that anywhere in France.'

'But you said there isn't enough,' said Grunwald.

'If the price is right, we'll find enough,' said the small, bald man.

'What is the right price?' asked Grunwald.

There was another quick conference, and the fat man told him. It seemed a lot.

'Cash,' added the small, bald man.

'I shall want credit,' said Grunwald.

There was yet another quick conference, with the decision that a fortnight's credit would cost him an extra ten percent.

'And what is being offered as security?' asked the young, flabby man.

'The security of the French Republic,' said Grunwald.

As he said it, he realized that he was probably committing an indiscretion, but he had the excuse that he had consumed a considerable amount of *eau-de-vie*, which was reacting unfavourably with all he had drunk the night before. In any case, Picard had offered no explanation of this unusual purchase, and it wasn't easy to get such a large amount of credit in a strange town, especially in a trade of which one knew nothing.

'The Republic?' echoed the fat man. 'Where's Aristide then?'

'Yes,' demanded the other two. 'Where's Aristide?'

'Er – I don't know Aristide,' said Grunwald.

'Don't know Aristide?' said the small, bald man. 'He's been handling all the salted cod buying for the government as long as I can remember. Has he got rumbled then?'

'Rumbled?' asked Grunwald.

'Let's talk plain,' said the fat man, taking charge. 'If you're taking over Aristide's job, are you coming in on the same terms?'

'What did Aristide buy salted cod for?' asked Grunwald. 'I mean, what did the government want it for?'

'The army, of course,' said the fat man. 'Isn't that who you're buying it for?'

'But of course,' said Grunwald. 'The army.'

'If you're new to the game,' said the fat man, 'you'd better learn the facts of life.'

'Tell him,' said the flabby young man.

'There's two kinds of salted cod,' continued the fat man, 'There's salted cod for eating and there's salted cod for selling.'

'Tell him the difference,' said the small, bald man.

'Salted cod for eating is in prime condition,' said the fat man. 'Like that piece there.' He pointed again to the nearest slab, from which the mongrel's urine still dripped. 'Then there's the other kind, which has gone mouldy, which is just for selling.'

'But it's good enough for the army,' said the flabby young man.

'Aristide would pay the price for the eating kind, but he'd take the selling kind,' said the fat man.

'And we'd split the difference,' said the small, bald man.

'I see,' said Grunwald.

The three members of the cod salting trade leaned forward eagerly : it was obviously their wish that the old arrangement should continue.

Grunwald revolved the matter quickly in his mind. Basically, he was an honest man, but it seemed clear that to conform with established custom would save both time and argument. 'We shall not quarrel, messieurs,' he said. 'Now, where are you going to get the extra merchandise?'

'There's no problem,' said the fat man. 'There's always plenty of the mouldy stuff about – but we might have a bit of trouble getting enough boxes.'

Picard hadn't said anything about boxes, and obviously he wanted the stuff quickly, so Grunwald said, 'I don't want it in boxes.'

'No boxes?' The three vendors looked at each other.

'Aristide always had it in boxes,' said the flabby young man.

'It's liable to deteriorate further without boxes,' said the small, bald man. 'Some of it'll fall to bits.'

'No boxes,' repeated Grunwald.

'Just as you like,' said the fat man, with a sniff. He turned to the flabby young man. 'Get some horses and carts.'

'I want it sent up to the station,' said Grunwald. 'How long will it take you to load up?' He was thinking that an hour or two on his bed would be acceptable.

There was a silence. 'Aristide always helped us to load,' said the small, bald man.

'It's to the advantage of all of us to cut costs,' said the fat man. Grunwald sighed, and took off his jacket.

Peyronnet was another with a hangover. Having played a leading part in the reconstruction of the crime, he had been lionized by friends and acquaintances, all of whom were eager to offer hospitality. He had also been suffering emotional stress from the brutal exposure of his love affair with the nubile Anne-Marie. One glass had led to another, and he had been in a poor state by the time he reached his bed.

However, his powers of recuperation were high because, as befits a lifeguard, he was in fair physical shape; indeed, he couldn't help being so, considering the number of miles he walked each day, either on the duckboards of the bathing establishment or the wooden floors of the restaurant Le Florida. Curiously, he had never been known to swim. Although he wore a bathing costume, the upper part of which was visible under his open white flannel shirt, he never actually ventured into the sea, and he had certainly never saved a life. To tell the truth, he hated the sea, which was much too cold for his taste. To salve his conscience, he occasionally reminded himself that he had once won a medal for swimming, but that had been at the age of twelve and in a heated, indoor pool.

He and Madame Berthier usually reached the establishment at about the same time in the morning. They both had a set of keys and the first one to arrive unlocked the cabins. She would open the pay booth, set out the change, count the towels and set the clocks which showed the times of the high tides as indicated in the local newspaper, while Peyronnet raked the sand, sluiced out the cabins and ran up the green flag which advertised the fact that, in his opinion, the bathing was safe. On days when the sea was so rough that it was obvious that nobody in his senses would bathe, he ran up a red flag, then sat in one of the cabins reading a novel by Victor Margueritte or Paul de Kock.

As Bonpain had already noted, it was a grey morning and there would be little business done in either of Peyronnet's activities, with only a small sum to write in his red notebook.

The establishment was in a mess. Trampling feet had kicked sand everywhere, and a dissident visitor had scrawled 'Hang All Policemen' in red chalk on the white paint of the pay booth. Peyronnet saw, with a start of guilt, that he had omitted to lock up, and was thank-

77

ful that it was a morning on which he had arrived before Madame Berthier.

He rolled up his trouser legs, filled a bucket with cold water and went to work. He liked to start with the ladies' cabins, because there was sometimes an interesting piece of lost property to be found, such as an item of underwear or a letter or, on one memorable occasion, a full-length nude photograph of Monsieur Galissard, the well-known local bookseller – and Madame Galissard certainly never bathed.

He began in the end cabin, the one by the canvas screen, the one in which he had been carrying on with Anne-Marie when they had been observed by the monstrous Madame Apelbommel. A smile hovered round his lips as he remembered the warm delights of the young girl's body. He gave the cabin a gentle mopping but did not sluice it down : he could not pour cold water on such precious memories.

By contrast, the next cabin, the one that had been occupied by the tight-lipped Dutch woman, received three buckets of water, flung into it with all his force, as if he were flinging it into her teeth. It was not a very satisfying gesture, because the third bucketful hit a far corner at an awkward angle and ricochetted back, soaking him from head to foot.

The next cabin had no particular associations for him and he gave it a competent, if disinterested, going over.

The door of the fourth cabin did not open easily and he had to push it hard. This frequently happened, because the doors were of unseasoned wood and warped easily. On this occasion, however, it was something inside the door which denied him ingress – something on the floor. He put his head round the half-opened door, and then dropped his bucket and mop with a clatter. He gave an anguished moan and staggered back, holding his head in his two hands.

Madame Berthier, who was turning the hands of the 'high tide' clocks to 10.57 and 11.23 respectively (although few would think of bathing so close to midnight) looked up in alarm and curiosity. In her turn, she poked her head into the cabin. Her reaction was to scream, lengthily and loudly and piercingly. She then ran along the duckboards and up on to the promenade, where she grasped one of the stanchions of the railings very firmly, planted her feet apart and began to scream again, continuously.

The day's traffic had not yet built up, and her screams carried a long way. Even in Monsieur Fallu's pharmacy, two hundred metres away in the Rue Théogene-Bouffart, a customer had to be asked to

78

repeat an order, and in the restaurant Le Florida, less than thirty metres away, a brandy glass was shattered.

In the commissariat, both Bonpain, on the first floor, and Verdi, on the second, rushed to the windows and, seeing the distressed Madame Berthier in full cry, tore downstairs and across the road. As the younger and spryer, Verdi was slightly in front as they reached the screamer, but Bonpain elbowed him aside.

Madame Berthier offered no further information than a shaking and pointing finger, so Bonpain and Verdi ran down on to the duck-boards. It was now Peyronnet's turn to point, and the two policemen hurled themselves at the door he indicated.

They suffered the same shock of déjà-vu already experienced by the lifeguard and the proprietress: there, lying on his back, his eyes staring sightlessly at the roof, was the man who had been murdered three days before. Yet was it the same man? True, he had the same pasty, plump face, the same small moustache, the same silk shirt and white jacket and trousers and handmade shoes, and the same green handkerchief protruded from his breast pocket, but half the moustache was hanging loose on a strip of gauze ... it was the unfortunate Inspector Gibeau, who had given such a successful impersonation at yesterday's reconstruction, and the obvious cause of death was a small but adequate stiletto buried between the third and fourth ribs, just to the right of the sternum.

The first to speak was Verdi, who said, 'I don't know who's going to play Gibeau in the next reconstruction.'

'There's no doubt about it,' said Bonpain. 'It's a woman's weapon.' He tossed the stiletto on to his desk.

'Whoever the killer was,' said Inspector Lautier, 'the sad fact is that he or she was wearing gloves.'

'Where's Dr Perchepied?'

'Still on the beach, *Monsieur le Commissaire*.'

'Until he gives us an approximate time of death, there's not much we can do.' Bonpain was tense and white. Although Gibeau was probably the worst policeman he had ever encountered, he had been one of his own men, and he felt a vague and indefinable sense of guilt that the inspector should have come to such an end while under his command. From a selfish point of view, too, the killing was upsetting, as a reminder that every policeman's job is a dangerous one and, but for the grace of God, it could have been Bonpain himself at the receiving end of the stiletto.

'I've talked to as many as possible of the men who were concerned with yesterday's reconstruction,' said Lautier.

'Yes?'

'As you know, there was very little for them to do once you and the friend of your brother-in-law had gone off to the restaurant Le Florida.'

'Me and who?'

'The friend of your brother-in-law, *Monsieur le Commissaire*.'

'Oh – yes.' Bonpain had completely forgotten the security cover under which Picard had introduced himself.

'That was at about half past four. At that time, Gibeau was chatting with a number of colleagues, including Verdi and Hanoteau. I was myself sitting in the pay booth. You'll remember that I brought you Madame Berthier and Peyronnet, and then the Dutch lady.'

'Yes.'

'It was then time for the day shift to go off duty and, as you had given me no instructions to the contrary, I suggested that routine matters should proceed as usual.'

'You did right, Lautier.'

'Gibeau was on the day shift, of course, but nobody remembers seeing him come back here.'

'So everybody drifted off, and nobody bothered to lock up.'

'That was Peyronnet's responsibility, *Monsieur le Commissaire*, and not ours.'

'I'm aware of that, but somebody should have had a look round to see that everything was all right before we left.'

'Perhaps Gibeau was doing that, *Monsieur le Commissaire*.'

'Possibly, but it wasn't his job.'

'I accept the rebuke, *Monsieur le Commissaire*,' said Lautier, respectfully, while saying to himself: 'The old devil! He was drinking away in Le Florida, and he could quite well have had a look round himself.'

Dr Perchepied entered. Above his grey beard, a strip of adhesive plaster bore testimony to the strength of Picard's punch.

'Come in, *Monsieur le Docteur*. What's your news?' Bonpain stood up to receive him.

'Do you want the technicalities?'

'No, just the time of death.'

'Between sixteen and eighteen hours ago. That's as accurate as I can be.'

Bonpain looked up at the clock. 'So it could have been at about the time he should have been leaving the beach – say, five o'clock.'

'It could well have been.'

'And if anybody had bothered to look round at that time we should have had a much better chance of catching the murderer. Anything else to note?'

'As was obvious, death was due to a stab wound.'

'Administered from the front?'

'To have struck with that amount of force, yes. The weapon was buried up to the hilt.'

'Would there have been a spurt of blood?'

'Not necessarily. The stiletto went in so far that it would virtually have closed the wound.'

'So it is unlikely that the assailant would have been marked.'

'There are no bloodstains on the walls to give that impression.'

'Could the assailant have been a woman?'

'A strong woman, or a woman labouring under passion. Is there anything else?'

'No, thank you, *Monsieur le Docteur*.'

'I presume an autopsy will be called for in due course.'

'Naturally.'

'I'd remind you that I have still to carry out the autopsy on the man who died on the beach the other day. You'll remember that I was about to undertake it at the time of the unfortunate assault by the friend of your brother-in-law.'

'Ah yes, most unfortunate. Has he sent you a letter of apology?'

'Yes. I was incapacitated for forty-eight hours, you know.'

'I hope you will send him a bill.'

'I have.' Doctor Perchepied bowed, and Lautier opened the door for him to leave.

'Where's Verdi?' asked Bonpain.

'Upstairs in the office.'

'I want him.'

Verdi was writing out his report of the morning's events. In his view, that which was written and placed officially on file could not be ignored, and he had known many cases in which thunder had been stolen by superiors because of a lack of written depositions.

81

'Verdi,' said Bonpain, 'you seem to have struck up a beautiful friendship with that woman.'

'With Madame Berthier?' queried Verdi, in puzzlement.

'No, you fool, the opera singer.'

Verdi's eyes sparkled. '*La divina*,' he said.

'We now have two murders bearing a woman's trademark,' said Bonpain. 'I want to see her.'

'She sings Lakmé again tonight, *Monsieur le Commissaire*.'

'If she's been a good girl she does; I want to know where she was yesterday. Go and get her.'

'At once, *Monsieur le Commissaire*,' Verdi departed eagerly.

Lautier put his head round the door. 'Monsieur Grunwald to see you,' he announced. He was holding his head in an unusual manner, as if keeping aloof from an unpleasant smell, which was exactly what he was doing.

'I can only give him a minute,' said Bonpain.

Grunwald entered, surrounded by as high a concentration of the smell of salted cod as it is possible to achieve outside the laboratory. He had spent the entire morning loading the mouldering slabs into four large carts which, when full, he and his three new associates had driven in procession to the station, where Picard, whom he had kept informed by telephone, was waiting. Several more bottles of *eau-de-vie* had been consumed, and Grunwald was unsteady in body and confused in mind.

Instead of congratulating him on his perspicacity and hard work, Picard had complained about the length of time he had taken, told his associates to unharness the horses and remove them, and taken Grunwald for a drink, which was the last thing he needed.

'We're loading the stuff after dark,' Picard told Grunwald, 'and I had no idea it would smell like that.'

'Do you want those three men back here?'

'No.'

'Do you mean we have to load all that stuff on the train by ourselves?'

'Yes.'

'Why?' It was the question he had been wanting to ask all the morning.

It had then occurred to Picard that he hadn't taken his colleague into his confidence, so he explained Lavigny's plan for smuggling the royal corpse back to its native land. The wagon would be attached to a goods train which left at midnight.

'Do we load the body too?' asked Grunwald.

'Of course. That's why the loading must be done after dark.'

Picard had looked at his watch. It was well after midday. He knew that Ernestine stayed in bed late on days when she was to give a performance, and it would be pleasant to join her before she got up. He wished it were possible to arrange for her to join him in his own hotel room, because hers was singularly untidy and distressingly dusty, but discretion had to come first.

'There are two jobs for you, Grunwald.'

'May I go and have a bath first?'

'I'm afraid not. Go and see Commissaire Bonpain, as soon as he's back from lunch, and tell him to take the Morals Squad off the vice probe and put them on to checking any young foreigners in town who appear capable of climbing up the front of a building.'

'Very well.'

'Then ask him for the key to the cellar underneath the fish market, and for the address of the boy who assists the police surgeon. You'll pay the boy a suitable sum to help you load HM's body on a hand-cart, and you'll bring it to me at the railway station as soon as it's dark.'

'Aren't you going to help?'

'I have other things in mind.'

So here was Grunwald at the commissariat to carry out his instructions. 'I have some messages from the friend of your brother-in-law,' he told the commissaire.

Once again, Bonpain had to adjust his mind to encompass his fictitious relative. 'Well?'

'He requests that the Morals Squad should be taken off the vice probe and put on to checking any young foreigners in the town who seem capable of climbing up the front of a building.' Considering the amount of alcohol he had consumed, he was proud of having delivered the message in an almost word-perfect manner.

The reaction of the commissaire was not encouraging: he smote himself on his forehead with both hands. Dear God, he had two murders on his hands, one of a king and the other of one of his own policemen, and here was this interloper from Paris demanding a full-scale investigation into the placing of chamber pots on the tops of public buildings. 'Thank you,' he said, with admirable self-control. 'Is there anything else?'

'Yes, I'd like the address of the boy who assists the police surgeon.' Which one of the two men from Paris fancied that spotty-faced young idiot? he asked himself. 'Get it from Inspector Lautier,' he said. Apparently he was expected to be a procurer now.

'And may we have the key of the cellar underneath the fish market?'

'What for?'

'I gather it's an instruction from Paris,' said Grunwald cautiously. Eager to get rid of his visitor and the smell of salted cod, he asked no more questions and took the key from a drawer.

'Thank you, *Monsieur le Commissaire.*'

'Thank *you,* Monsieur Grunwald.'

Fifteen minutes later, Inspector Verdi brought in Ernestine. She was handcuffed to him. Once again, Bonpain smote his forehead. 'Idiot! I told you to bring her here, not arrest her.'

Startled, Verdi fumbled for the key of the handcuffs. As on the first occasion, it meant almost dragging Ernestine's hand into his trousers pocket. It was most disturbing.

Very sweetly, Ernestine said, '*Monsieur le Commissaire,* will you be very kind and put through a telephone call to Paris for me? It's to the Minister of Justice.'

Bonpain went almost on his knees with contrition, and anxiety to keep the minister out of it. Never did a commissaire apologize more profusely.

'Another thing,' said Ernestine, looking accusingly at Verdi, 'he stood and watched me while I dressed.'

'But I have seen you *undress* so often, madame – as Desdemona in *Otello,* and as Zerlina in *Fra Diavolo,* and as Princess Saamcheddine in *Marouf.*'

'I've never played Saamcheddine,' said Ernestine.

'Then it was another singer almost as lovely,' said Verdi.

'You're a dear man,' said Ernestine. 'You can come and handcuff me as often as you like.'

Now that the ministerial danger seemed in abeyance, Bonpain moved into action. He picked up the stiletto and tossed it on to the desk in front of Ernestine. 'Ever seen that before?' he asked.

Ernestine looked at it casually. 'Yes,' she said.

'You have?' queried Bonpain, startled at her admission.

'Yes.'

'When?'

'Yesterday.'

'Where?'

'In the Opera House.'

'Whereabouts in the Opera House?'

'On the stage.'

'Please explain.'

'After Lakmé, I sing Madame Butterfly. Yesterday afternoon, I was rehearsing.'

'With this stiletto?'

'At the end of the opera, Madame Butterfly stabs herself. Have you never seen it?'

' "O Death, take thou my heavy heart" ' sang Verdi. 'Surely she stabs herself with her father's sword, which bears the inscription "To die with honour when one can no longer live with honour"?'

'In this Opera House,' said Ernestine, 'you stab yourself with whatever you can get your hands on. I'll bet that tatty stiletto has sufficed for every Butterfly, Tosca, Juliet, Don José, Ernani and Edgar who has played here for the past fifty years.' She held out her hand to Bonpain. 'I'll give it back to them.'

'You certainly won't,' said Bonpain. 'Just in case you don't know, it was the weapon used in a murder yesterday.'

Her laugh was silvery and almost mocking. 'Oh, *Monsieur le Commissaire*, you haven't had *another* murder.'

' "See how villainy encompasses me around" ', quoted Verdi. 'I *due Foscari*, Act II.'

'That's enough, Verdi,' snapped Bonpain.

'Wherever did you see I *due Foscari*?' asked Ernestine. 'No opera house ever has the courage to put it on.'

'At La Baule,' said Verdi. 'When I was a boy. They did *L'Africaine* as well.'

'Verdi!'

'I'm sorry, *Monsieur le Commissaire*.'

'Madame, I wish for a full and detailed account of your movements yesterday afternoon and evening.'

'Certainly. I received a convocation to take part in a reconstruction of the crime at three o'clock. You may remember, as you were in the next cabin to me, that I arrived on time, and you may also remember that I adopted the identical state of dress ...'

'We needn't continue with that,' said Bonpain, feeling himself flushing bright red. 'You left early.'

'With Monsieur Picard's permission.'

'Did you go immediately to the Opera House?'

'As soon as I'd got my clothes on. They had an old woman from the chorus standing in for me.'

'That would be Madame Prendtout,' said Verdi. 'Rumour has it that she was Massenet's first mistress.'

'I always thought there was something odd about Massenet,' said Ernestine.

'May we continue, Madame?' asked Bonpain patiently. 'Did you rehearse the scene where you stabbed yourself?'

'We walked right through the whole opera, cutting the arias and duets: we'll work on those tomorrow.'

'What did you do with the stiletto when you had pretended to stab yourself?'

'I let it fall to the stage.'

'And it stayed there until the end of the opera?'

'It is the end of the opera,' said Verdi, 'except for the tenor coming on to take the child.'

'And you should see the child,' said Ernestine. 'Eleven years old and mumps.'

'Who picked up the stiletto?' asked Bonpain.

'I couldn't tell you,' said Ernestine. 'I didn't.'

'What time was it?'

'About five-thirty.'

'Who is responsible for looking after such weapons in an opera house?'

'In any responsible opera house, the property master: in this Opera House, anybody who hasn't anything else to do.'

'Who handed it to you in the first place?'

'I've no idea. Someone in the chorus, I think.'

'What did you do after the rehearsal?'

'I went back to my hotel.'

'Who saw you?'

'Plenty of people. I had a cup of coffee in the lounge.'

'Check that,' said Bonpain to Verdi. 'And then?'

'I met Monsieur Picard for dinner.'

'At the hotel?'

'We dined at Le Jockey, in the town. Avoid the shellfish.'

'Did you go back to the beach at any time?'

'Of course not.'

'Did you stay with Monsieur Picard for the rest of the evening?'

'He left me about half an hour before midnight; he had an appointment.'

'A meeting at the *mairie*, I presume,' said Bonpain, hoping to find out something about the occasion from which he had been excluded.

'He didn't take me into his confidence. You may or may not know that Monsieur Picard undertakes professional tasks which may be of a confidential nature.'

'I do know,' said Bonpain, bridling a little. Really, it was shameful the way nobody gave him credit for being in the confidence of the powerful.

'May I go now?' asked Ernestine.

'First, you will please go upstairs and dictate a full statement to Inspector Verdi.'

'"Hand me the pen, and I will sign the warrant of my death",' carolled Verdi. '*Don Carlos*, Act IV.'

'And then, Verdi,' continued Bonpain, 'as you seem to know so much about the workings of the Opera House, you will go there and take a full statement from everyone who was present at the rehearsal yesterday afternoon.'

'There won't be anybody there until tonight's performance,' said Verdi.

'Then take the statements before the curtain goes up.'

'There won't be time, *Monsieur le Commissaire*.'

'Then make time. If necessary, hold up the performance.'

'Hold up the performance?' repeated Verdi, shocked at the very idea.

'And from now on, Madame,' continued Bonpain, 'you will account to me for all your movements.'

'It would be simpler if I could account to Monsieur Picard,' said Ernestine.

'To me, please.'

Verdi escorted Ernestine from the room. Soon, from the inspectors' office upstairs came laughter and the singing of operatic excerpts.

In the meantime, Picard had presented himself at Ernestine's door and knocked incessantly. He was amazed when, on enquiring at the reception desk, he was told she had already gone out. Philosophically, he sought his own bed and slept soundly.

87

That was what Grunwald would have liked to do, but he spent a frustrating afternoon tracking down the pimply-faced boy who assisted Dr Perchepied. The boy's name, it appeared, was Leopold LaChevre, and his medical duties were only a part-time occupation. He had a number of other part-time occupations and they all seemed to have a vocational link: he was a part-time butcher's boy, a part-time assistant to the local taxidermist and, in the high season, he was a part-time guide to the dungeons and torture chamber in the ruined castle which stood on the cliff to the east of the town.

Grunwald tracked him fruitlessly through the latter three part-time occupations, which involved visiting a number of cafés in search of information. He had decided that *eau-de-vie* was a little heavy for daytime drinking, and was taking a little absinthe for his stomach's sake. He eventually found the boy at a matinée performance of a German film called *The Massacre of Glencoe* at the Ciné-Palace, and made a rendezvous with him for seven-thirty. Next there came the task of hiring a suitable handcart, which he was able to do from a painter and decorator. He parked it outside a brasserie while he had a modest meal of snails, fried scallops, veal cooked in a cream sauce, salsify, a large slice of *chameaucrotte*, and some strawberry ice-cream. He washed it down with a bottle of white Macon and, in view of the unpleasant task he was to perform, a large glass of armagnac.

It was now time to wheel the handcart, which was equipped with a tarpaulin suitable for covering a body, to the fish market. Seeing that the small café frequented by the porters was about to close, he took another precautionary glass of armagnac. He had some difficulty in inserting the key into the lock of the barred gate: having succeeded, he left the gate ajar for the boy.

One thing which Grunwald had not queried was what lighting was provided, and he spent some time standing on the slimy stairs lighting matches and peering about for a source of illumination. At last, he discovered a hand lantern in a niche in the wall. He lit it and swayed cautiously down the stairs.

The dual use of the cellar as mortuary and a store for fish boxes was not entirely satisfactory, as he found when he put his foot in a discarded box lying in the passage and found that it was stuck. He could release it only by leaning back against the damp wall and striking his box-enclosed foot repeatedly on the ground, which was tiring. It took a minute or more of hard banging.

He advanced under the archway. The feeble light from the lantern

88

showed a shrouded form lying on a table. Sternly suppressing a trembling of his knees, he raised the lantern and moved closer. He pulled back the shroud. He was at the wrong end: it was the royal feet. He edged sideways and tried again. His Majesty had never, during the days when Grunwald had so ineffectually guarded him, impressed him as being an inspiring-looking man, and the days in the cellar had not improved him. Grunwald let the shroud fall back into place.

The trembling of his knees was becoming harder to control, but fortunately he had thought to slip a flask of cognac into his hip pocket. He took a long draught. The trembling ceased, but an annoying attack of double vision took its place. He closed his eyes and shook his head to clear it.

Upstairs, he heard the shuffle of feet. It would be the boy. He moved back towards the archway to light the way for him, but then he stopped. There were voices – two voices. One was asking what had become of the bloody lantern.

Grunwald retreated, blowing out the flame. He backed, as cautiously and accurately as his alcoholic state permitted, to the rear of a pile of boxes and crouched behind them. In setting down the lantern, he scraped it on the floor.

'What's that?' asked one of the voices.

'Flaming rat,' said the other.

'If there are rats down here, don't they eat the stiffs?'

'I expect they do – but the stiffs don't complain.'

The two men seemed to be carrying a burden, because there was heavy breathing.

'I wonder who left that gate open.'

'One of the market people; there's nothing down here worth pinching.'

'Light the gas, before we break our flaming necks.'

There was a scratch of a match, and then a faint glow which burst into the yellow-green glare of gaslight. It was the same colour as salted cod, recalled Grunwald, with distaste.

There was some shuffling. Grunwald protruded his head. He could see little of the men, who were against the light and with their backs to him, except that they wore some kind of uniform. One of them half turned, so he hastily withdrew.

'Let's get out of here.'

'Is that market café still open?'

'No, it'll be closed by now.'

'The one by the post office should be all right.'

'Sod the bastard who stole that lantern.'

The gaslight was turned out, and two pairs of heavily shod feet clumped towards the archway.

As soon as they had gone, Grunwald took another drink. Where the hell was that boy? He relit the lantern.

His double vision was now giving him real trouble: quite clearly, he could see two shrouded forms. The illusion was so real that he moved closer. He pulled back the shroud: there was His Majesty. He pulled back the other shroud: there was His Majesty. He gave a little strangled moan. This was it! Many times he had reproached himself for the amount he drank, and had made ineffectual resolutions to cut down. Now he was paying for his sins. Here was madness. Here was delirium tremens at last.

There were footsteps down the stairs, light, youthful, accustomed footsteps. The boy came under the arch.

'Good evening, Monsieur Grunwald.'

Grunwald swayed, shuddered, said nothing.

'I see you've got a handcart outside.'

Grunwald nodded. His head was reeling, his stomach was liquefying with fear. At such an early age, he was finished – a pathetic, crazed, useless man. He had a good degree and he spoke four languages. He had been kind to his mother and not unattractive to women. Now he was unemployable, unwanted, an object of pity and derision.

'Is this the one, Monsieur Grunwald?'

The boy had hold of the shoulders. Grunwald nodded again. He took the legs. They bore the stiff, shrouded figure to the archway, and up the stairs.

'You're useless, Grunwald,' said Picard.

Grunwald didn't argue; he agreed.

'We gave you a king to look after, and you let him get murdered. All right, that's understandable: anybody can lose a king, and I didn't utter a word of reproach – but to turn up pissed on a job like this! There's a report going into head office about this that'll have you out of the service in seconds. You're a disgrace.'

Grunwald wanted to say 'yes', but he merely turned away to be sick. It was the eighth time he had been sick since he arrived at the railway station.

He had paid off the boy outside the fish market and had pushed the handcart all the way himself. It had taken a long time, because he had been going from one side of the road to the other, and all the strength seemed to have left his legs. When he reached the station, Picard had been standing in the middle of the road waiting for him. Making due allowance for his double vision, Grunwald had directed the handcart to the left-hand side of the left-hand image, but somehow it had still hit Picard in the stomach.

'The way things are going, it'll take us most of the night to do this job,' said Picard.

They had laid the body of His late Majesty on the floor of the railway wagon, respectfully, with his hands crossed on his chest, and covered him with a first layer of salted cod. Now, laboriously, they were unloading the flattened fish from the horse-drawn carts into the handcart, pushing it sixty or seventy metres along the track and loading it into the railway wagon.

'And that'll mean we shall miss the midnight train,' continued Picard, 'and there isn't another until tomorrow night.'

Grunwald longed for a drink, and lovingly fondled the flask in his hip pocket. Then he pulled himself together and, to put temptation from him, threw the polished silver flask into the railway wagon with the next load.

A few minutes later, a hideous thought wormed its way from the murky recesses of his muddled brain. He was concerned in a matter of a murdered king and it was quite possible, if anything went wrong, that some foreign hands would search the wagon for clues. In such an event, the searching hands could hardly miss the flask, which would be generously daubed with Grunwald's fingerprints. As a professional, if minor, practitioner in international intrigue, he knew that his fingerprints were on file, as a matter of course, in many countries. If those fingerprints were identified, there would be no question of a diplomatic enquiry into his guilt but the simpler process of putting his name on a short list of those to be assassinated. He developed a new symptom: a cold sweat.

The handcart was loaded again, and he and Picard pushed it over the soggy, wet surface beside the track. Grunwald climbed up into the wagon, bruising his shins for the twentieth time, and Picard began throwing greasy, stinking, salted slabs for him to stack. He ignored the rain of the revolting objects and scrabbled wildly among those beneath his feet.

'Grunwald, what are you doing? Get on with it.'

He said the first thing that came into his head. 'I'm being sick again.'

'You repulsive, drunken pudendum. You're a disgrace to your race, and I'll report you to the Chief Rabbi. To be drunk on active service is a capital charge: they'll take you down to Vincennes and put you in front of a firing squad.'

At that moment, Grunwald would have welcomed a firing squad, but he continued to search, desperately. How could he have been so foolish as to discard the incriminating flask? – and the delicious, life-saving fluid that was inside it?

'You can't still be being sick,' came the stinging voice. 'Your miserable little body couldn't hold all that. Here – stack this.' A flung cod caught Grunwald on the left ear, knocking him sideways, which was a merciful thing, because his right hand, thrown out to restore his balance, alighted on the flask.

'It's all right, Picard, I'm better now.' The cod rained in fast and hard, but Grunwald ignored them: he was going to have a drink, and he didn't care what it did to him. He put the neck of the flask, rimmed with rotten fish, to his lips, and swallowed the entire contents.

'How much did you pay for this stuff, Grunwald, because to me it smells putrid.' Picard's voice went remorselessly on. 'Is this the stuff you Yids call *gefülte* fish?' Picard's abuse was getting more and more racist. There was still considerable prejudice in government circles, and Grunwald remembered with a shiver the misery he had gone through in his schooldays when the Dreyfus affair had been at its height. But a miracle was happening. The deep draught of cognac had caused a warm glow in his stomach, banished the feelings of sickness, and the blood began to course in his veins: his headache vanished, the aches disappeared from his limbs, his vision cleared. 'Send them up faster,' he shouted. 'A few years on the Pyramids would have taught you goyim how to work.'

The load was stacked in a matter of seconds, and Grunwald sprang down to earth and pushed the empty handcart back along the track at the double.

'Christ!' said Picard.

Thanks to Grunwald's rejuvenation, the wagon was padlocked and ready in good time to be attached to the midnight train. Having sent him to return the handcart, Picard went back to the hotel to scrub himself in a hot bath, change every stitch of clothing, and apply a discreet touch of Houbigant's 'Coeur de Jeanette' to his armpits. He arrived at the Opera House to see the curtain come down on the last act of Lakmé.

He stood in the wings and watched Ernestine and the tenor taking calls in response to tepid applause from a scattered house. A large bouquet was handed up to her, and she expressed delighted surprise. A similar bouquet was handed up to every prima donna at the end of every performance, and was returned to the florist the next morning.

Behind the backcloth, a sweating Verdi had lined up a group from the chorus: he had forbidden them to leave the theatre and was taking statements. Picard, who as yet knew nothing of the second murder, eyed the procedure with mild curiosity.

Ernestine came over to him and slipped her arm into his. 'It's the same in every opera house in the world,' she said. 'If I gave a few francs to the leader of the claque and the man who operates the curtain, I could have as many calls as I like.'

'How did it go?' asked Picard.

'I'd rather sing to this audience than wash dishes, but it's a close thing.' She steered him towards her dressing-room. Dressers were not provided, so he helped her out of her sari and into a peignoir. The dressing-room, he noted, was deplorably dusty.

Two elderly opera-goers presented themselves at the door, bringing a programme for Ernestine to sign. They had seen Lakmé many times and, with no effort, they recalled the casts and dates, but they had no apparent critical sense and remembered neither the quality of the singing nor the staging: they collected operas as they might have collected stamps.

Ernestine got rid of them as quickly as possible, and they were succeeded by two young Englishmen in beautifully cut evening clothes. Their cards had been brought in by the stage-door keeper, and bore the names Lord Sherrington and the Hon. Anthony Preacham. They were both tall and thin and had fair hair brushed very flat. They were almost interchangeable except that His Lordship had more nose and the Hon. Anthony less chin.

They explained that they were cousins, were making a tour of Europe to complete their education, that they had been enraptured by Ernestine's performance and that they had accorded themselves the honour of expressing their homage. They seemed disconcerted to see

Picard in the dressing-room, and it was obvious that their intention had been to invite Ernestine to supper, with the hope that they would also be joined by one of the other ladies in the cast.

'A most remarkable performance,' said Sherrington.

'Yes, wather,' said his cousin.

'We never expected such a musical treat.'

'No, wather not.'

They were, however, critical of the British army uniforms worn in the opera. (This was not surprising as they had been made originally for a long-forgotten production of *The Daughter of the Regiment*, and served for military garb of any period and any nation.)

The two cousins then exchanged glances and presumably decided that, as they had money to spend and time to spare, they had little to lose, so Lord Sherrington said, 'We should be very honoured, Madame, if you would care to take a little supper with us.' Turning to Picard, he added, 'Naturally, Monsieur, we hope that you will join us.'

It was now the turn of Ernestine and Picard to exchange a glance. Neither of them had eaten that evening, and neither had any objection to eating at the expense of rich young Englishmen on a European tour. 'You are most kind, My Lord,' said Ernestine. 'We should be delighted.'

'Most kind,' echoed Picard.

'Splendid,' said Sherrington. 'Where would you like to go? There is always the Grand Hotel of the Baths and of Serbia, where we are staying.'

'It's not very gay there,' said Ernestine. 'There is a solemn hush which is more suitable to a national library.'

'Or the Hotel of the Loire and of the Golden Chariot?'

'It is where I am staying,' said Ernestine, 'and I am the only guest under the age of eighty.'

'There is a restaurant of which we have heard, Le Jockey.'

'The clientele is younger, but the food is quite uneatable.'

'Then, Madame, you must make a suggestion.'

'Usually after a performance we go to the Café des Colonnes. The food is ordinary but honest, and the atmosphere is cheerful.'

'Then that is where we shall go. Is it far – because we did not bring our car.'

'It's only three minutes walk, and the exercise will do us good. Give me a few moments, and I'll join you at the stage door.'

The two young men bowed their way out, and Ernestine sat at her dressing-table to complete her toilet.

'I was looking forward to having supper with you alone,' said Picard.

'You'll be sleeping with me alone, and that should be good enough. Anyway, we needn't talk to them, just let them pay the bill.'

'You're a hard little thing,' said Picard.

'Not with my friends, as you well know.'

The Café des Colonnes was even fuller than usual, and Ernestine received her usual round of applause when she entered. The two Englishmen showed obvious pride and delight in being in her company. They were shown to the best table, and Ernestine sat facing the room, waving and blowing kisses to colleagues from the Opera House and townspeople whom she knew by sight. The meal was good, the wine was better, and Ernestine proved to be a delightful guest, teasing her hosts but also seeming to take a genuine interest in the adventures they had had on their travels.

One of the other tables was occupied by a noisy family party, celebrating an anniversary of some sort. One of the party was Inspector Verdi, who was pressed to go to the piano. Obviously, he had a local reputation as a pianist, because people at other tables took up the cry. With a suitable show of reluctance, he seated himself at the upright Pleyel, and showed himself to be an amateur pianist of a very good standard indeed. He began by playing a selection of popular French tunes of the day, interpolating those called for by his audience. He then played two or three Italian tunes, which were greeted with delight by members of his family, and then he paused and looked round the room. A fat commercial traveller with cropped hair, sitting alone in the corner, was obviously German, so Verdi played for him a few tunes from his homeland. There was still a strong anti-German feeling in the town because within living memory – on Saturday, 10 December 1870, to be exact – an occupying force of eight thousand Prussian troops had marched in, had remained for six months, and had demanded and received 647,243 francs as a contribution towards their expenses. However, the fat commercial traveller had been a frequent visitor for a number of years and was now tolerated, so there were no protests. The German further cemented international relations by sending the pianist a bottle of wine.

Verdi again looked round the room. 'Are you English?' he called out to Lord Sherrington and the Hon. Anthony, a question which

95

produced a general laugh, because it was hard to imagine their being anything else.

'Wather,' said the Hon. Anthony.

Verdi played a selection of English tunes, including 'The Boers Have Got My Daddy', 'The British Grenadiers' and 'Pale Hands I Loved'.

'He seems a well-travelled man,' said Picard, who was a well-travelled man himself.

'He's lived in five countries,' said Ernestine. 'His family exports spaghetti.'

Verdi paused, flexed his fingers, and then struck the opening chords of the introduction to 'One Fine Day', looking pleadingly towards Ernestine. There was a ripple of anticipatory applause.

'Please, Madame,' said Lord Sherrington.

With a smile, Ernestine walked gracefully to the piano. Verdi improvised the accompaniment well, leaving her to sing alone those phrases in which he was not sure of her *tempi*.

When she had bowed to her applause, she and Verdi put their heads together to decide on an encore. Rejecting the 'Bell Song' from *Lakmé* as too much like hard work, she chose the '*Valse Ariette*' from Gounod's *Roméo et Juliette*, for which she received a standing ovation.

Verdi took her by the hand and led her back to her table. The manager, brushing past her, whispered, 'There will be no bill for your party tonight.'

'Oh yes there will,' replied Ernestine, 'but I'll be happy to eat for nothing tomorrow night.'

'That man played really well,' said Picard, when Ernestine had seated herself.

'He's a nice person,' said Ernestine. 'We get along splendidly together. He was very apologetic about putting the handcuffs on yesterday.'

'Yesterday?' queried Picard.

'I was arrested again. Haven't you heard?'

'Indeed I haven't. What for?'

'Murder, as usual.'

'I thought the police were quite satisfied; why did they want to talk to you again?'

'This was about the new murder.'

'There's been another one?'

'Oh yes, didn't you know? You are out of touch.'

'Who? When?'

'On the beach, yesterday afternoon. I'm told it was a policeman.'

Picard jumped to his feet. 'I must find Commissaire Bonpain,' he said. He turned to his hosts. 'Thank you, Lord Sherrington, for a most enjoyable meal.'

'A pleasure – and please call me Sherry, my dear chap; everyone does.'

'I should be honoured – and perhaps you'd care to call me Chanteloup.'

'But of course.'

Picard turned and bowed to the Hon. Anthony. 'My thanks to you also, Monsieur.'

'Gweat pleasure.'

'I must ask you two gentlemen kindly to see Mademoiselle Thibault back to her hotel. I have to leave you on an urgent business matter.'

Where he was to find Bonpain at so late an hour he did not know, but he would go to the commissariat and have someone fetch him : in Picard's view, when a man was serving his country's interests, he gave up his right to sleep. Fortunately, however, he ran into *Sergent de Ville* Maupas, who told him that he had seen the commissaire going into a café opposite the stage door of the Opera House.

At the bar of the café, Bonpain was talking to Monsieur Drach. Picard took him by the arm and drew him aside. 'Why wasn't I told?' he demanded.

'Because nobody has seen you,' said Bonpain.

'Tell me now.'

Bonpain told him all he knew : it wasn't much.

'Any suspects?' asked Picard.

'I'll be very surprised if it wasn't that singer.'

'I'll be very surprised if it was.'

'I had your message about putting the Morals Squad on to chivvying foreigners.'

'Did you do it?'

'Obviously not, with these new developments. Murder must come first.'

'But this is the same case, man.' Picard told Bonpain about the mysterious climber with a taste for song. 'It was the same song the Dutchwoman heard from the adjoining bathing cabin.'

Bonpain scratched his chin. 'It could have been the same malefactor who put the pink chamber pots on the roofs,' he said.

97

'What pink chamber pots?'

Bonpain imparted more information.

'The *mairie*, the brothel, the church, the commissariat,' ruminated Picard. 'What do the fingerprints show?'

'What fingerprints?'

'The ones on the chamber pots.'

'Until a few moments ago, that matter was no more than a drunken escapade.'

'So you have no fingerprints.'

'Obviously not.'

'You see now the importance of chivvying foreigners, as you call it.'

'But I didn't then, did I?'

'Where are the chamber pots now?'

'I let my men take them home. I have to keep them in good heart; hardly any of them have slept in three nights.'

'Let's make it four. Is there only one man questioning the Opera House staff?'

'Tomorrow, I'll have them all at it.'

'It should be done at once.'

'I'm doing a bit myself now.' Bonpain indicated Drach. 'That's the manager.'

The stage-door keeper ambled in and spoke to Drach. 'Somebody's put one of those things on the top of our roof,' he said, in a loud voice.

'One of what things?'

'Pisspots.'

'Good!' said Picard, who had overheard. 'That's the first good news today.'

'I'm glad you think so, who ever you are,' said Drach, in a surly tone. 'So far as I'm concerned, it's just more expense to get the thing brought down.'

'I'll get it done for you for nothing,' said Picard. He turned to find Bonpain, but Ernestine appeared at his elbow.

'I hope you're having a good time in here,' she said.

'I'm sorry I rushed away, my sweet. I'll be with you in just a moment.' He grabbed Bonpain. 'I want the fire brigade.'

'What for?' asked Bonpain. He raised his hat to Ernestine.

'Of course, you know the commissaire,' said Picard.

'Quite intimately by now,' said Ernestine. 'He keeps having me arrested – and yesterday we were in adjoining cabins at the reconstruction.' She added the latter part of the sentence for the pleasure of watching Bonpain go bright red.

'What do you want the fire brigade for?' asked Bonpain again, to change the subject.

Picard pressed money into Ernestine's hand. 'Go and buy some drinks, my love.'

'What sort of drinks?'

'Buy a selection, and then I'll make up my mind.'

Ernestine went to the bar. 'What do you want the fire brigade for?' asked Bonpain, for the third time.

'There's a chamber pot on the roof of the Opera House.'

'There wasn't this afternoon; I had a man inspect all the high buildings in the town.'

'That's good, it means that our climber is still at it and that the evidence is fresh. Get the fire brigade at once.'

Bonpain shook his head. 'Not tonight.'

'Why not?'

'They're playing a belote tournament with the Harmonic Society.'

'Then they'll have to break it off.'

'But they've been getting chamber pots down all day.'

'Fine. They should be in good practice.'

'It's dark now.'

'It was dark when somebody put it up there.'

'Surely it'll do in the morning.'

'Bonpain, I want the fire brigade – now.'

Bonpain sighed. 'They started the tournament at seven o'clock; they'll have had a lot to drink.'

'Drunk or sober, Bonpain – the fire brigade.'

'They won't like it,' said Bonpain, as he made his way to the telephone.

They didn't like it. When the call came through to the Café des Sports, where the tournament was being held, the proceedings were building to an exciting climax.

'I'm afraid I have to ask your co-operation in an urgent matter,' said Bonpain to the fire chief.

'A major conflagration?'

'Not exactly.'

'A disaster?'

'Not really.'

'A flood?'

99

'No.'

'You intrigue me.'

'It's another chamber pot.'

'Another – ?'

Bonpain fancied he could hear the fire chief's jaw drop. 'It's on top of the Opera House.'

'And you want it done now?'

'At once,' Picard muttered into Bonpain's ear.

'At once,' echoed Bonpain.

'You can go and – ' began the fire chief. Then he remembered that he was only three years away from his retirement and that he had always wanted a gold watch, so he said, 'Very well, Commissaire.'

Ernestine had used the money Picard gave her to buy drinks for Monsieur Drach and the stage-door keeper, so Picard had to start a new round.

'Are we going back to bed early?' whispered Ernestine.

'Not yet,' he replied. 'I have to wait for a fire engine.'

He had to wait quite a long time, because the firemen had to make their way from the Café des Sports to the fire station, and then they had to change into their uniforms, and then it took the usual ten minutes to get the engine started – and, as Bonpain had surmised, they had had a lot to drink by now.

The appliance clattered to a halt outside the stage door of the Opera House, and an admiring crowd collected to watch the fire fighters climb down cautiously to the ground.

Bonpain greeted the fire chief with a warm handshake, but the fireman's lips remained set. 'Show me the object,' he said.

The stage-door keeper was called, and he pointed to the pot, hanging rakishly on one of the spiked uprights of a decorative wrought-iron fence which ran along the apex of the roof.

'And please don't put any fingerprints on it,' asked Bonpain.

'How do you suggest we manage that?'

'By wearing gloves,' suggested Bonpain, 'and when you've got it, you can pop it in a bag.'

'What gloves? What bag?' asked the fire chief.

The problem was put to the stage-door keeper, who opened the Opera House wardrobe and produced a pair of mailed gloves worn by a crusader in I Lombardi, and the sack in which Rigoletto put his daughter's body. In the meantime, the folding ladders had been unfolded as far as they went, and it was discovered that they would take a man to within six or seven metres of the apex of the roof. After that, he would have to improvise.

The fire chief lined up his men and inspected them. Legrand was the best climber but also the most drunken, so he was passed over for Ory, who was a poor climber but suffered from a liver complaint which kept him from anything stronger than shandy.

After handshakes from his comrades and an encouraging cheer from the crowd, Ory set off aloft, with a coil of rope over his shoulder, the sack tied round his waist and the mailed gloves glittering on his hands. When he ran out of ladder, he had to throw the rope to lasso the spiky fence. It was a long throw, and he had to make a number of attempts, to mounting criticism and advice from below. Possibly owing to his liver complaint, he was not an even-tempered man, and he gave as good as he got, shouting down abuse and defiance.

Slowly, he hauled himself up towards the fence. The proprietress of the café was most affected by the personal risk he was running, and professed that she couldn't look. 'It isn't right for a man to risk his life for a chamber pot,' she said. 'My brother-in-law can get them wholesale for only four francs each.'

'He's a brave man,' said Monsieur Drach. 'He shall have a couple of free tickets for *Madame Butterfly*.'

Hand over hand, Ory hauled himself up the rope. The iron fence did not look too secure in its cement setting, and he was careful to keep the weight he put on it as constant as he could. There was a cheer from below as he grasped the fence and swung himself along it to retrieve the pot. He grasped it by the handle and lifted it free.

Now came the most difficult part, to release the sack from around his waist and open the top of it widely enough to slip the pot inside. For this, he needed three hands.

He moved along another few metres to a brickbuilt chimney stack and steadied himself against it, rising to his feet. He placed the pot on the top of the stack, and moved his hands down to his waist to deal with the sack.

'He's going to have a piss,' shouted a raucous voice from below, and there was loud laughter.

Stung to anger, Ory raised his fist and shook it at the crowd. In doing so, his arm caught the chamber pot and it disappeared down the chimney.

There was more laughter. Picard cursed in despair.

'Fish it out, Ory,' shouted the fire chief.

Ory dutifully pulled himself up by the arms so that he could see down the chimney. Then he shrugged, and shook his head. 'It's gone all the way down,' he shouted.

'What do you know about your chimneys?' Picard asked Monsieur Drach. 'Are the flues straight?'

'No, they go off at all angles,' said Drach.

'Then I want a chimney sweep.'

'Wouldn't do you any good. We use gas for our heating, and all the flues are bricked up at one point or another. You'd have to pull the whole theatre down to find that pot.'

'Then let's do that,' said Picard.

There was a sudden smell of second-hand shellfish, and two poached-egg eyes looked into his. 'Bloody good effort, those pisspots, what?' said Colonel Withers.

'Good effort?'

'I'll bet you anything you like they were put up by Cambridge chaps.'

'Why do you think that, Colonel?'

'Well, night-climbing's a Cambridge speciality, isn't it? All the best climbers are Cambridge men. I wasn't bad at it myself, in my day. I've hung a pisspot or two on the pinnacles of King's – and I'd have got one on the top of Trinity if the bulldogs hadn't spotted me.'

'Bulldogs?'

'Coves in top hats – university rozzers. The Opera House is easy, anybody could have done that, even a climber from the other place – but the *mairie*'s a tough climb.'

'You're right there, Colonel.'

'Best thing I ever saw was when some chaps managed to stick a growler on the roof of the Senate House. Can't imagine how they did it, because it took dozens of men to get it down. I'll tell you, only Cambridge chaps would have the nerve to stick a pisspot on top of the commissariat. I wish I knew who the fellers were; I'd buy them a drink.'

Friday, 12 September

The next day was long and hard and unproductive. It began early. Picard slipped from Ernestine's arms at daybreak and returned to his own hotel, where he roused Grunwald. They were at the commissariat before Bonpain arrived. Picard ordered that a reconstruction of the reconstruction should be arranged for the afternoon. Then the three of them locked themselves away to talk the case through.

Inspector Vaquin, of the Morals Squad, brought in a list of the younger foreigners known to be in the town, each of whom had been vetted as to the likelihood of his having the physical capability to climb the front of a building. Bonpain arranged that surreptitious fingerprinting should be undertaken and enquiries made as to their movements during the hours when the night-climbing was done.

'Why are you so confident that we're dealing with a foreigner?' asked Grunwald.

'Can you imagine any Frenchman being fool enough to do such a thing?' replied Picard, mildly.

The reconstruction of the reconstruction was a failure. Whereas the original reconstruction had been based on people's movements at an exact moment, on this occasion there was no exact indication as to when the stabbing had taken place, so little could be done except to take statements, which could afterwards be laboriously interlocked. Peyronnet insisted on re-enacting the discovery of Gibeau's body but, because nobody volunteered to play the role of the corpse, it was represented by a stuffed dummy.

In the middle of the afternoon, Gibeau's family arrived in the form of two elder sisters who kept a wool shop in Poitiers. They had not seen their brother for many years, nor had they communicated with him, because a policeman was not a class of person with whom they ordinarily cared to associate, but they were loud in their protestations that they were entitled to very considerable financial compensation for their loss – and where was his watch?

At one point, when Bonpain and Picard were standing alone together by the pay booth, the commissaire looked down at his feet, cleared his throat, and said, 'Monsieur Picard, I appreciate that you're working on this case on a higher level, but it's becoming increasingly difficult for me to work efficiently if I'm not kept in the picture.'

'My dear Commissaire,' Picard's tone was shocked. 'I assure you that nothing is being kept from you except the knowledge of a few diplomatic moves which must remain secret. You'll appreciate that when a king has been murdered on French soil, then a powder keg has been opened, and the fewer people who have matches to strike the better.'

'I suppose so. It has been reported to me that certain top-level meetings, in which you have been involved, have been held in this town.'

'If you've heard that, it means that our top-level secrecy is not good enough. What more have you heard?'

'Nothing more than I've told you, except that the meetings have been held under armed guard.'

'Who told you that?'

Bonpain was tempted to expose the mayor, but he was too nice a person to do such a thing. He merely said, 'It's my job to know everything that goes on here, and I have my informants.'

'Of course you have, Bonpain. I know that, together, we're going to crack this case, but there must be calm decisions, and sometimes those decisions must be dictated to us. Have patience.' He patted the commissaire reassuringly on the arm.

At six o'clock, he went to see Colonel Withers, who admitted that the king had been away so long now that he was worried. Picard thought of the royal corpse, encapsulated in salted cod, being rumbled along some branch line in his native land.

Whereas the fact that the king had been murdered was still known only to Bonpain, Picard and Grunwald, plus a few officials in Paris, the murder of Inspector Gibeau could not be hushed up, and there was an influx of senior policemen. As there were obvious difficulties for them in working on a case about which most of the facts could not be revealed, Picard sent a coded message to Lavigny and arranged to have them recalled at once. Bonpain was duly grateful.

With a weary shrug of the shoulders, the commissaire said, 'I don't think there's much we can do now, except go through the routine motions and wait for something to happen.'

Saturday, 13 September

Something happened on the afternoon of the following day: there was an urgent message for Picard at his hotel. It read, 'Warrior will telephone you four o'clock at place of previous meeting.'

Warrior was Lavigny's code name, so Picard walked to the *mairie* just before the appointed time and knocked at the door. Being Saturday afternoon, the building was unstaffed, but he was admitted by the same uniformed soldier who had been there on the previous occasion. He went upstairs to the mayor's parlour, sat in the mayor's chair, put his feet on the mayor's desk and waited.

The telephone rang. 'Devious?' That was Picard's code name, and the voice was Lavigny's.

'Yes.'

'The goods you despatched by rail – '

'Yes?'

'They arrived at their destination early this morning.'

'That was quick.'

'We expedited matters as far as the frontier.'

'Of course.'

'Our representative who received the goods has been in touch.'

'Good.' Picard waited for a word or two of congratulation.

'He is very angry, and so am I. The wrong goods were despatched.'

Picard was puzzled for a moment, then he remembered his own reservations about the salted cod. 'You mean it wasn't the top quality?'

'I mean it was the wrong consignment.'

'But I loaded it myself, with Reckless' – 'Reckless' was Grunwald's code name. 'Do you mean we should have filled the wagon with the stuff, right to the top?'

'It was what was at the bottom of the wagon which has dissatisfied our client.'

A hideous suspicion smote Picard. 'The wrong one?'

'The wrong one.'

'Oh, sod it!'

'It was a bad mistake, Devious.'

'I think I know how it happened.'

'Excuses are not required.'

'I'll send him the right one.'

'Very quickly, Devious.'

'Very.'

'What would you like our dissatisfied client to do with the wrong one?'

'Anything he likes.'

'It would be tidier if he returned it to you, just in case you need it.'

'But not in the same ballast, please.'

'Obviously not; that commodity is not exported from his country to yours: it will probably be a load of chemical fertilizer.'

'Addressed to me?'

'Naturally. It will arrive on Monday morning.'

'Warrior –'

'Yes?'

'I'm very sorry.'

'Your new load will be on the goods train leaving at midnight, won't it, Devious?'

'Warrior, that gives us no time at all.'

'Your new load will be on the goods train leaving at midnight, won't it, Devious?'

'Yes, Warrior.'

'It had better be.'

There was a click as Lavigny replaced the receiver. Picard ran out of the room and down the stairs. The soldier was waiting in the hall.

'Do you have transport?'

'A motorcycle, Monsieur.'

With Picard on the pillion, the motorcycle puttered off to the Grand Hotel of the Baths and of Serbia. Grunwald was not in his room, nor in the bar. Taking up a precious twenty minutes, the two men searched the town. They found their quarry in the Restaurant of the Golden Cock, where the fish soup was admirable but the sauces too highly seasoned.

Grunwald was dragged bodily from his chair and called seventeen unkind names by Picard as he pulled him outside on to the pavement. He was told in explicit terms of the hideous mistake he had made, a mistake unparalleled in the history of the service to which he belonged . . . and that immediately after losing a king who had been entrusted to his care! At once, he was to find the pimply-faced boy who assisted the police surgeon; he was to find his three acquaintances in the cod-salting trade; he was to deliver four cartloads of first-grade salted cod, together with the right royal body, to the railway station in the shortest time possible. In the meantime, Picard would make a more modest contribution by fetching the handcart and by arranging for a goods wagon to be at their disposal and attached to the train leaving at midnight. They would co-operate in loading the wagon.

The next seven and a half hours were the hardest in Grunwald's life, and very disagreeable ones for Picard. The only salted cod which Grunwald's acquaintances were able to provide at such very short notice on a Saturday afternoon was so mouldy that it had been put aside as useless even for selling.

At two minutes to midnight, Picard slammed shut the sliding door of the wagon and padlocked it. Blue-clad railwaymen then pushed the wagon along the track and hitched it to the goods train. As on the previous occasion, mysterious orders had arrived from a very high quarter that the midnight train must leave on time even if no other did, so it was away barely more than fifteen minutes late.

Picard and Grunwald, panting and exhausted, watched the train go. There was a pile of salted cod which they had not had time to stuff into the wagon. Grunwald happened to be standing with his back to the pile. Picard pushed him into it.

'On Monday morning,' said Picard, looking down at him, 'there's a wagonload of chemical fertilizer arriving. You will unload it – all on your own.'

'Very well,' said Grunwald, miserably.

'The object you find concealed inside you will take back to the place where you originally found it.'

'I'll need help to get it down the stairs.'

'You can slide it down – and you can clean the object up, too.'

Grunwald fought back a desire to burst into tears.

107

Ernestine was bored and more than a little angry. She realized that Chanteloup Picard had a job to do, but if she had known that it would take up so much of his time she would have started a liaison with someone more readily available – perhaps with Monsieur Blanc, the artistic director of the Opera House, whose looks were pleasing and whose professional associations might one day prove useful, or with the bass who had sung Milakantha and was now singing the Bonze and who was old but interesting, or even with the opera-loving police inspector who kept arresting her.

She had sung her first performance as Butterfly, conscious of the empty box she had reserved for Picard. Afterwards, feeling disinclined for the camaraderie of the Café des Colonnes, she had called at the Grand Hotel of the Baths and of Serbia to see if he had left a message for her. He hadn't, so she wandered into the lounge where, at her entrance, the string trio broke into an excruciatingly played selection from the opera she had just sung. She ordered sandwiches and opened a copy of *La Vie Parisienne*, but it was a dull issue, full of drawings of women in their underclothes making coy remarks to chubby cupids whose private parts were hidden, in a highly unlikely manner, by their quivers. She switched her attention to a back number of the local paper, in which considerable prominence was given to a statement by the Bishop of Verdun that the tango was profoundly dangerous to morals.

Into a cane chair at the next glass-topped table to her right sank a lady of about the same age as Ernestine, but as dark as Ernestine was fair. With an imperious wave, she summoned a waiter and ordered a pot of tisane.

'It's Carmen herself,' said Ernestine.

The dark lady turned and bowed. 'Now that the season advances, the management engages artistes of star stature.'

Ernestine smiled sweetly. 'In this town, if the management billed Melba, Tetrazzini and Caruso, the inhabitants would think it was a juggling act.'

'With what are you delighting the audience, Ernestine?'

'I'm sure you must have seen the posters in the foyer of the hotel, Cécile.'

'Oh yes, I seem to remember. *Madame Butterfly*, isn't it?'

'I sang the first performance tonight.'

'Did it go well?'

'Exceptionally well. A full house, and we were cheered to the echo.'

'I'm told that you were paid an unusual tribute; that they decorated the roof in your honour.'

'It's better to have them hung on the roof than thrown at you,' said Ernestine.

'I'm sorry I didn't come to see you, my dear. As you know, Madame Butterfly is one of my own great rôles.'

'I saw you in it – at Chalons-sur-Saone.'

'Ah yes. Afterwards, the students unhitched the horses from my carriage, and drew me through the streets themselves.'

'To the river?' asked Ernestine. 'When do you start rehearsing Carmen?'

'Tomorrow, if you can really call them rehearsals. I sing the first performance the following day.'

'When did you arrive, Cécile?'

'I've been here several days. I had some time between engagements and I thought I'd spend it by the sea.'

'I haven't seen you.'

'I've been resting.'

'Are you staying in this hotel?'

'I am.'

'I hope someone is paying the bill.'

'It would be a very poor business if somebody wasn't. How is Monsieur le Ministre?'

'Strictly between ourselves, Cécile, he's terribly boring.'

'Is he here?'

'He's in Paris. He says we've very likely going to have a war.'

'He's probably organizing one. Politicians are the only ones to do any good from them.'

'He says all that scrapping in the Balkans may boil over, and the Germans are being far too militaristic.'

'I've never liked the Kaiser . . . but the King and Queen of England went to see him – at that wedding. That may have helped.'

'Don't you believe it; they're cousins – and family fights are always the fiercest.'

'I must say I like the idea of singing La Marseillaise to cheering crowds from the steps of an opera house.'

'And I'll bet that if the Prussians had stayed in Paris in 1871, they'd have put on a better opera season than the French ever have.'

'Darling, it's treason to say things like that.'

'Are you still with the baron?' asked Ernestine.

'No, I've moved on.'

'Upwards, I trust.'

'Always – and rather considerably in this instance.'

'Well done.'

'He's upstairs, asleep. They must have their sleep.'

Ernestine became aware that two chairs at the glass-topped table to her left were now occupied, and that the occupants were nodding and bowing in her direction. She turned, and saw Lord Sherrington and the Hon. Anthony Preacham, resplendent in white tie and tails.

'Dear lady,' said Sherry, 'you were magnificent.'

'You were in front?'

'Indeed we were; we wouldn't have missed it tor worlds.' He rose to kiss her hand. The Hon. Anthony contented himself with a toothy grin. 'May we have the honour of inviting you and your charming companion to join us.'

'Join you in what, dear Sherry?'

'A little champagne, don't you think?'

'It shouldn't do us any actual harm.'

'Will you present us to your friend?'

Ernestine presented the two young gentlemen to Madame Cécile Lanchon.

'Enchanted, dear Madame,' said both the Englishmen.

Champagne was brought, with sweet biscuits. Anthony went to sit on the other side of Cécile.

'Did you see *Butterfly* tonight?' Sherry asked Cécile. 'It was one of the greatest operatic experiences of my life. To my mind, Mademoiselle Thibault is the finest soprano in Europe.'

'Everyone is entitled to his opinion,' said Cécile.

'Madame Lanchon is also a singer,' said Ernestine.

'How interesting,' said Sherry. 'And, of course, if she knows a little about it, she can appreciate your worth.'

'I'm not sure about that,' said Ernestine.

'I used to listen to Ernestine when I was very young,' said Cécile. 'I used to say to myself that one day, unless I worked very hard, I might sound like that.'

'Dear Cécile,' murmured Ernestine.

'Dear Ernestine, what an inspiration you were to me.'

'Top hole,' said Anthony, making his first conversational contribution to the evening.

'Tomorrow night, she sings Butterfly again,' said Sherry. 'If she had her rights, all the crowned heads of Europe would be here to applaud her.'

'At any rate, we'll have you here, My Lord,' said Ernestine.

'And I'll clap and clap until my hands are sore.'

'So shall I,' said Anthony.

'I see the following production will be *Carmen*,' said Sherry. 'It'll be a hard task for the leading singer to follow the divine Thibault.'

'I agree,' said Ernestine.

'Have you any idea who it'll be?'

'It'll be me,' said Cécile. 'They couldn't get Emmy Destinn, and Geraldine Farrar wanted too much money.'

Sherry tittered. 'I say, I seem to have put my foot in it.'

'Wather,' said Anthony.

'These two gentlemen are making a grand tour of Europe,' confided Ernestine to Cécile.

'How interesting,' said Cécile, stifling a yawn.

Sherry told two boring stories about Como and one about Pisa. Anthony began to tell a story about a donkey he had seen near Athens, but he lost interest and tailed off.

'Where were you before you started your tour?' asked Ernestine.

'We were at university.'

'What were you reading?'

'English.'

'I can never see the point in studying your own language. What'll you do when you get back?'

'We've both got family estates to look after in due course,' said Sherry. 'Money's a big responsibility, don't you think?'

'Certainly,' said Ernestine and Cécile together, taking considerably more interest than before in their two companions.

'Have you a lot?' asked Cécile.

'I haven't as much as he has,' replied Sherry, with a glance at Anthony. 'He owns half Wiltshire.'

'But that's not so much fun as owning half Piccadilly, which you do,' said Anthony.

'Yes. I'm very fortunate to have that. I've often thought I'd like to build an opera house in Piccadilly.'

'A wonderful idea,' said the two ladies, enthusiastically.

'Do you know England?' asked Sherry.

'Intimately,' said Cécile, who had once accompanied an elderly Hungarian count to Cheltenham to take the waters.

'Not as well as I should like,' said Ernestine, who had played for a week at the Alhambra, Leicester Square, in a French *scena* called 'Oo, La la!', singing *'Ma Normandie'* while the dancers changed into Normandy peasant costumes, *'Mon P'tit Soldat'*, while they dressed themselves as Zouaves, and leading a chorus of *'Aupres de ma Blonde'* when they all appeared in nightgowns for the saucy finale.

'How about a dwive?' suggested Anthony.

'Where to and in what?' asked Ernestine.

'There's an *auberge* about six miles inland where you can dance by candlelight,' said Sherry. 'Very romantic and all that.'

'I've heard of the place,' said Ernestine. 'We'll come on the strict understanding that we stay downstairs.' She looked enquiringly at Cécile, who nodded. Ernestine knew that Chanteloup Picard would be annoyed, and that suited her very well; it would serve him right for leaving her alone so much.

'Anthony has a magnificent new Lanchester,' enthused Sherry. 'It goes like one o'clock.'

'And that's just the time we're going to be home,' said Cécile. 'Not a minute later.'

'And let's have no nonsense about running out of petrol on the way back,' added Ernestine.

'I always keep woller-skates under the seat,' said Anthony, giggling.

They strolled out into the foyer. Several parties were assembling to go to the casino, while the Duc d'Aramanthes stood alone and thoughtful by a potted palm.

'Forgive me, I must buy a newspaper,' said Sherry. 'I backed a couple of nags at Longchamps this afternoon.' He crossed to the magazine stand, while the others waited.

Anthony's pale, finely-chiselled nostrils quivered. 'By Jove,' he said, 'what a perfectly ghastly smell. They must be having fearful twouble with the dwains.'

The smell became stronger as Chanteloup Picard approached from the entrance. From a distance, he looked almost his immaculate self, because he had removed his jacket while loading the wagon, and he had been into a café to wash and clean himself as well as he could. Several people whom he had passed by the glass doors had handkerchiefs to their noses.

'Ernestine, my love,' he said, as he took her hand and kissed it. 'Forgive me for my absence, I've been terribly busy.'

Loyally, Ernestine controlled her features. 'This is Monsieur Chanteloup Picard,' she said, presenting him. 'Madame Cécile Lanchon.'

'I'm most honoured, Madame.' Picard kissed Cécile's hand. 'I've heard you sing on a number of occasions, and always with the greatest pleasure.' Surreptitiously, Cécile rubbed her hand on her scented furs.

'You already know Mr Anthony Preacham,' said Ernestine.

'Indeed.' The two men shook hands, Anthony standing well back.

'Madame Lanchon is to sing Carmen,' said Ernestine.

'I've already heard you in the rôle,' said Picard to Cécile. 'It must have been seven or eight years ago – in Étretat.'

'That would have been at the very beginning of my career, and I think it could only have been four or five years ago.'

'I'm sure you're right,' said Picard, gallantly.

'It was an ambitious production for a small town, with a real horse in the last act.'

'Not a very well behaved one,' remembered Picard.

'Alas, no,' said Cécile, then giggled. 'All over Escamilo's foot.'

Sherry was reading his newspaper as he came towards the group. His nostrils were less finely-chiselled than Anthony's but they were more mobile, and their fluttering was more obvious. He looked up in distaste. Picard removed his hand from Ernestine's arm, on which he had placed it in a proprietorial manner, in order to greet him.

'Did you win, Sherry?' asked Ernestine.

'But of course; I don't need the money, so I always win.' He retreated a pace or two backwards.

'Have you been fishing, Monsieur Picard?' asked Cécile.

The question was based on a reasonable deduction and was asked in all innocence, but it confirmed Picard's suspicions that he was smelly.

'I'm going upstairs to bath and change,' he said to Ernestine. 'I shan't be long.'

'Don't hurry, because we four are going out for a drive,' said Ernestine, brightly.

'I see.' As she had anticipated, Picard was piqued.

'Anthony has a new Lanchester.'

'Really.'

'It's a Bwitish car,' said Anthony, proudly. 'It has a four-cylinder 3,299 cc engine with preselector epicyclic box.'

'How splendid.' Picard turned to Ernestine. 'Wrap up well.' In addition to being piqued, he was suddenly dog-tired and was feeling distressingly self-conscious. He looked round at all four faces, nodded curtly, and moved away towards the lift.

'Is he angry?' asked Sherry.

Ernestine shrugged.

'Shall we go?'

Anthony's Lanchester was gleaming and spotless; even the wire spokes of the wheels were polished, and it started at the first swing of the starting handle.

Sunday, 14 September

It had now become a daily contest between Commissaire Bonpain and Chanteloup Picard as to which of them was first to reach the commissariat in the morning. Obviously, even on a Sunday Bonpain considered it his duty to be in his office to receive the man from Paris, while Picard, who was a poor sleeper, ordinarily liked to start his day's work as early as possible, and especially after such a night of pique and jealous misery as he had just spent. This morning, he beat Bonpain by twelve minutes.

He sat morosely in the office while routine matters took their course: there was Lautier's morning report, which consisted of nothing but trivia, and Lautier was followed by Verdi, with a report on Ernestine's movements. With tightened lips, Picard heard that she and Cécile had not been returned to their hotels by Lord Sherrington and his cousin until 3.30 am.

At midday, nothing useful having been accomplished, and Bonpain having gone home, Picard telephoned the Hotel of the Loire and of the Golden Chariot, but Ernestine had given instructions that she was not to be disturbed.

He then went in search of Grunwald, whom he found having a leisurely luncheon at the Café des Colonnes. Having cursed him for being lazy and useless, he gave him the tedious and pointless job of compiling a list of all visitors to the town known to have patronized Madame Berthier's bathing establishment.

After his own lunch, which consisted of a *croque monsieur* and a whole bottle of Chambertin, he went in person to Ernestine's hotel, but she had gone out and left no message.

In the evening, having checked at the commissariat that there had been no developments, he changed into evening clothes and went to the Opera House to sit in the front row of the stalls at the second performance of *Madame Butterfly*, but although he applauded more loudly than anyone in the house, Ernestine did not even glance in his direction. When he went round to the stage door, he was told that she had already left.

He drank nearly half a bottle of cognac in a gloomy café in the main shopping street, and went to bed. It had been a lost day.

Monday, 15 September

When, the next morning, Picard listened to Verdi's account of Ernestine's movements, he heard that she and Cécile had again been out with Lord Sherrington and the Hon. Anthony and that, on this occasion, they had not returned until almost 4.30 am. For want of something better to do, and out of a vague sense of masochism, he asked for Vaquin's files on the two Englishmen. They made dull reading; the two men said that they were in the town for their health and instruction, and at the times when their movements might have been of interest they claimed to have been studying French in their hotel suite. Then came a piece of information which made Picard sit bolt upright. He swore gently to himself. Bonpain looked up.

'Anything of interest?'

'I'm not sure. I'm going to see the two Englishmen.'

'Vaquin's impression is that they're harmless.'

'He may be right.'

'Monsieur Picard, there's one thing I must ask you. Monsieur Grunwald came in and borrowed the key to the cellar of the fish market: he told me he was acting under instructions from Paris.'

'That's quite true.'

'Instructions that, of course, I hadn't been told about.'

'I'm afraid that's true too.'

'May I now please have the key back?'

'By all means. I don't have it with me.'

'I'll gladly send one of my men to collect it.'

'Don't worry, Grunwald will bring it in.'

'It concerns Inspector Gibeau's funeral, you see. His two sisters are here, and they're complaining that they're losing profits they should be making in their business in Poitiers, so they'd like the funeral as soon as possible.'

'Of course.'

'In fact, it's arranged for tomorrow.'

'Tomorrow?'

'Have you any objection?'

'No, no, none at all. I'll see that you get the key.'

'The undertaker might wish to do some work.'

'He might well,' agreed Picard.

'It'll be a police funeral, of course – with a flag on the coffin, and a volley fired by his comrades.'

'I'm sure it will be most touching; I shall be there.'

'Gibeau was far from being a good policeman, but his comrades liked him.'

'That's very important. May I take away these files on the two Englishmen?'

'Naturally.'

Grunwald was shaving when Picard threw open his bedroom door and stormed in.

'Good morning,' said Grunwald, apprehensively.

'The commissaire wants the key to the cellar of the fish market.'

'It's in my trouser pocket.'

'Is it now? Thank you for the information, Grunwald. And what happens if the commissaire elects to use the key? He goes down into the cellar, expecting to find two bodies – and what does he find, Grunwald? What does he find?'

'Bugger all.'

'Exactly. As you so pithily put it, Grunwald, he finds bugger all – and one of those missing bodies is to be buried tomorrow, with full military honours.'

'Military honours?'

'Police honours then. Inspector Gibeau is being laid to rest – and where is Inspector Gibeau?'

'Under a load of chemical fertilizer.'

'The undertaker will want to clean him up a bit, and, by God, he'll need a bit of cleaning up – in fact, I think I've told you to clean him up a bit yourself.'

'He should be back here soon.'

'Then you'd better go to the station and wait for him. Have the handcart with you, and rush him down to the fish market, then rush the key to the commissaire.'

'All right, that'll be one body, but we'll still be one short.'

'I have permission from Paris to let the commissaire into the secret of the disposal of His Majesty's body, as soon as we hear that it's arrived safely in Mittenstein-Hoffnung. But I certainly can't tell him that until we've got the wrong one back. Stop fiddling with your face and get to the station.'

'What do I do with all the fertilizer?'

'Anything you like, it's all yours.' Picard went out, slamming the door, and went down to the floor below. He knocked on the door of the suite occupied by Sherry and Anthony. He had to knock several times before Sherry's voice called, 'Who is it?'

'Chanteloup Picard.'

'Can you come back later, dear fellow, we're not up yet.'

'I want to talk to you now. Open up.'

'If it's about Ernestine, I swear to you that – '

'It's official business. Open up, or I'll have the door opened.'

'What a strange way to talk. Are you the police or something?'

'Or something.'

'Wait a minute.'

There was some muttering inside the room, and then the door was opened. Sherry had combed his hair and put on a blue silk dressing-gown, but Anthony was gummy-eyed, tousle-haired, and wearing crumpled pyjamas.

'Come in,' said Sherry. 'Can I offer you a glass of champagne?'

Picard shook his head. Anthony shuddered at the thought.

'My cousin is not in very good form this morning; he looked on the wine when it was sparkling. Are you quite sure you won't have a glass?'

'No, thank you.'

'It's nature's own restorative,' said Sherry, pouring some for himself. 'Some coffee, perhaps?'

'Let's get down to business.'

'Just as you wish. We thought you were a friend of Ernestine's; we had no idea you were a policeman.'

'I'm not a policeman.'

'You're acting like one, old horse. The police seem very active in this town; we had a chap round yesterday, asking the most impertinent questions.'

Picard sat down in an armchair and opened the files he carried

119

under his arm. 'I have here the answers you two gave to those questions, and I've never read such a lot of nonsense.'

'That's a very challenging statement,' said Sherry.

Anthony was sitting with his head in his hands, groaning quietly to himself. Picard turned to him. 'Were you in a fit state to drive a motor-car along country roads at 4.30 this morning?'

'So you know what time we got in,' said Sherry.

'I know a lot of things.' Picard turned back to Anthony. 'Answer my question. You had two distinguished singers as your passengers. You were risking their lives.'

'I got them here, didn't I? Anyway, they'd had a few glasses themselves, and enjoyed the ride.'

Picard went back to the files. 'It seems that, the night before last, you sat in here reading good books and thinking beautiful thoughts.'

'We're students,' said Sherry. 'That's what we're here for.'

'My information is that you're graduates.'

'True, but we still don't consider that we've finished our education; that's why we're on this trip.'

Picard looked down at the files. 'I see that you're both graduates of the University of Cambridge.'

'Lovely place. Ever been there?'

'No.'

'A symphony in stone, dear boy. You should see the willow-shaded river flowing past the backs of the colleges, the prettiest girls in England dancing at May balls ...'

'And some of the stupidest idiots in England risking their lives to stick chamber pots on the tops of buildings.'

There was a hush. Anthony gave an extra loud groan and said, 'We're rumbled.'

Sherry said, 'Look, Picard, in Cambridge, chamber pot planting is looked on as an innocent lark, a harmless jape. When that police inspector came to see us, he seemed to take it awfully seriously, and we thought – well, it's obvious that you French haven't got a sense of humour about this, so we denied it. Damn it, we're law-abiding, respectable chaps out for a bit of fun, and we didn't want to get hauled up in court before some beak and get our names in the paper. You see what I mean.'

'You see what he means,' echoed Anthony.

'Which one of you stuck a pot on the *mairie*?' asked Picard.

'I did,' said Sherry. 'Dead easy, that one.'

'I nearly broke my neck coming after you.'

'That was you, was it? You got in a bit of trouble with the overhang. Obviously, you need a bit of practice. Still, you did quite well as far as you went: you must be a fit man.'

'Lord Sherrington, do you remember what you were singing as you reached the top?'

'Singing? I'm not much of a singer. I leave that to the professionals.'

'You're fond of opera, aren't you?'

'Not very knowledgeable, but I like it.'

'You were singing "The Soldiers' Chorus", from *Faust*.'

'Possibly – although it's not one of my favourite operas.'

'I assure you it's a fact.'

'Is there a law against it then? What's all this about? We admit to planting the chamber pots; that's what you came about, isn't it? Now can we go back to bed?'

'No. Get dressed.'

'Why?'

'Because we're going down to the commissariat.'

'Can't it wait until later? Surely it's not a very serious crime.'

'Murder is.'

'Murder?'

'That's what I said.'

'Who's murdered who?'

'You're suspected of doing the murder, and if you did it, you'll know who the victim was.'

'Monsieur Picard, I'm not a killer. For God's sake, do I look like one?'

'I've seen some very unlikely looking killers. I mean, do I look like a killer?'

'Have you killed?'

'Indeed I have. Professionally, you understand – when authorized to do so.'

There was a tap at the door.

'Come in,' said Sherry. 'It'll probably be Arsène Lupin.'

Grunwald put his head round the door. 'Ah, there you are,' he said to Picard. 'I chased you downstairs, but the porter said you hadn't gone out, and a chambermaid told me she saw you come in here.'

'I should have taken more care, I don't usually alert chambermaids of my movements.'

'There was a telephone message from Warrior. He wants to talk to you. He'll telephone you in thirty minutes at the usual place.'

'Perhaps you'd like to tell these gentlemen where the usual place is, since you're telling them the rest of my business.'

'But I don't know where the usual place is.'

Picard sighed and made a hopeless gesture. 'Take Lord Sherrington down to the commissariat.'

'Lord who?'

'This' – Picard extended a weary hand – 'is Lord Sherrington.'

'How do you do,' said Grunwald.

Sherry bowed politely.

'This is not a social matter, Grunwald. He's to be held on suspicion of murder.'

'Just because I sang a song?' said Sherry, with a bewildered air.

'Just because you gave yourself away.' Picard went to the door. 'Don't let him get away,' he said to Grunwald, 'and, for God's sake, take the right one this time.'

There was the usual delay in getting a taxi started, so it was almost time for Warrior's call when Picard reached the *mairie*. The uniformed soldier was not on duty on this occasion, so Picard headed straight for the stairs. A porter stepped out of a side room and started to follow him, but Picard called out 'It's all right' in an authoritative tone, and kept going.

He knocked at the door of the mayor's parlour and went in without waiting for an answer. There was a fat man in the room, and Picard correctly took him to be the mayor. Apparently he had just been brought a cup of coffee, because it was steaming on the desk. The mayor was steaming a little too, because his hand was down the front of the dress worn by the young female member of his staff who numbered coffee-making among her duties.

'You don't know me, *Monsieur le Maire*,' said Picard, ignoring Tinville-Lacombe's confusion. 'I'm one of the men who have been using this room on certain occasions. You know what I am referring to?'

'Yes – yes, Monsieur.'

'I'm expecting a very important telephone call.'

'Please – please make yourself at home. My name is Tinville-Lacombe.' With a view to the hoped-for decoration, he decided that it was important to announce his name, although the embarrassing incident with the young woman would probably not count to his credit: or perhaps it would, he said to himself, brightening, because it showed that despite his bulk he still had virile interests. 'I'll leave you, Monsieur.' He hoped that the unknown visitor would reveal his name, but he did not. Tinville-Lacombe pushed the girl out of the room and followed her.

Picard sniffed disdainfully. He was all in favour of a man having a hobby, but the girl was far below standard, with a thick waist, sagging breasts and a squint. He sat down and, having carefully wiped the rim of the cup with a clean handkerchief, drank the mayor's coffee.

He waited for two minutes, during which time nothing happened except that a thin man with glasses knocked at the door and came in. Picard put out his tongue at him, and the man scuttled away. Then the telephone rang.

'Devious?'

'Yes, Warrior.'

'You ridiculous idiot, you've done it again.'

'Done what again?'

'Sent the wrong merchandise.'

'Nonsense.'

'Don't say "Nonsense" to me; I've just heard from our client.'

'Warrior, we've only got two, and he's had both of them now.'

'This one has a false moustache.'

'Then this is the wrong one.'

'So was the first one.'

'Nonsense, there's the right one and the one with the false moustache. If the one he's got now is the one with the false moustache, then the first one he had was the right one.'

'Don't keep saying "Nonsense" to me, Devious, or you'll find yourself out of a job; and I'm not sure that won't happen anyway. Sort yourself out.'

'Yes, Warrior.'

'Find the right one and send it to you-know-who.'

'I haven't got any more, Warrior.'

'A right fool you'll look if we have a war and millions of people are killed and it's all your fault. I'd make quite sure you'd be in the front line on the first day.'

'I haven't got any more, Warrior,' Picard repeated, but the man at the other end had replaced his receiver. Picard continued to sit at the desk for some minutes, his mind revolving futilely round an insoluble problem. His eyes read, over and over again, an estimate for the construction of a new sewage plant at a cost of 700,000 francs. It did not seem enough, so he added another two noughts.

Tinville-Lacombe knocked at the door. 'Have you finished, M'sieur? I have a meeting of the Ways and Means Committee.'

Picard left the building, patting the mayor absently on the shoulder, a gesture which filled that official with joy. Walking at a puzzled pace, he went to the commissariat. He did not go up to Bonpain's office, because he did not want to answer any more questions about the key to the cellar of the fish market. Having ascertained that Grunwald had delivered Lord Sherrington, he set off at the same puzzled pace for the railway station.

He found Grunwald sitting on the goods-yard fence, staring at a pile of coal. 'The train isn't in yet,' he reported.

'I want to talk to you. Where can we get a drink?'

Grunwald brightened. In the absence of further symptoms of total alcoholic breakdown he had abandoned his project of becoming a teetotaller.

'The nearest place is down that street, but it's a bit aggy-daggy.'

'A bit what?'

'I mean, it's not very good.'

'Show me.'

They went to the dark little café, where the proprietor still had a dewdrop on the end of his nose. Grunwald's fat cod-salting contact was at the zinc bar. 'Want any more?' he asked.

'No,' said Grunwald, tersely.

The cod salter winked and moved away. Following the custom of the house, Grunwald bought two large glasses of the harsh *eau-de-vie*. Picard made no attempt to pay, which was unusual. They went outside to a single metal table set precariously on the uneven pavement. Picard flicked the dust from the slatted seat of his chair before he sat down.

Picard said, 'A right fool you'll look if we have a war, and millions of people are killed and it's all your fault. I'd make quite sure you'd be in the front line on the first day.'

'What have I done now?'

'You've done it again.'

'Done what again?'

124

'Sent the wrong one.'

'Nonsense.'

'Don't say "Nonsense" to me. I've just heard from Warrior.'

'We've only got two, and I've sent both of them now.'

'This one has a false moustache.'

'Then this is the wrong one.'

'So was the first one.'

'Nonsense, there's the right one and the one with the false moustache: if the one he's got now is the one with the false moustache, then the first one was the right one.'

Picard sighed. 'That's the way I look at it. Give me a pencil and paper.'

Grunwald searched in his pockets and produced a torn envelope and a chewed stub of a pencil.

'Grunwald, you'll forgive my saying so, but at the stage you have now reached in a career as urbane as ours, I'd expect you to produce a slim, gold pencil and a leather-bound notebook.'

Grunwald was tempted to say that a man at the stage he had now reached in a career as urbane as theirs would not expect to spend his time loading and unloading railway wagons full of dead bodies and salted cod and chemical fertilizer, but he held his peace.

'I'm going to work this problem out mathematically,' said Picard. 'Now, we have the King of Mittenstein-Hoffnung, a plump man with a moustache, who is murdered in a bathing cabin by a person unknown. Following local custom, His Majesty's body is deposited in the cellar of the fish market. You're with me so far?'

'Yes.'

'So we have the first body, the body of His Majesty. Let us call that Body A.' He wrote the letter A on the envelope. 'Right?'

'Right.'

'Then there is the body of Inspector Gibeau, a man of about the same build, who was dressed to look like His Majesty, and who wore a false moustache, and who was also murdered in a bathing cabin by a person unknown. Right again?'

'Perfectly.'

'Let us call that Body B.' He wrote down B, beside A. 'Now, if the second body you sent them was the one with the false moustache, as they say it is, then it was Body B.'

'So the first one I sent them, without the false moustache, was

Body A, which was the right one, which is what I've been saying all along.'

'So there are two alternatives – '

'There are no alternatives,' interrupted Grunwald. 'I did my job the right way, which is the way I always try to do it.' His air was righteous.

'So there are two alternatives,' repeated Picard, as though Grunwald had not spoken. 'Either our man in Mittenstein-Hoffnung was mistaken, or Body A wasn't the right one.'

'If Body B wasn't the right one, then Body A must have been,' insisted Grunwald, obstinately.

'But let's suppose that the first body wasn't that of His Majesty after all.'

'It looked like His Majesty.'

'So did the second one.'

'Then whose body was it?'

'That's what I'm going to find out.' Picard scraped back his chair and stood up. 'It's time you went to the station to fetch Body A.'

'May I have my pencil back?' asked Grunwald.

Picard went in search of Colonel Withers. He was not difficult to find; he was enjoying a dozen oysters generously spattered with tabasco, on the terrace of the Café des Colonnes.

'A word, Colonel,' said Picard, sinking into the next chair and indicating to the waiter that he would like a dozen of the same. 'The time has come for plain speaking.'

'I applaud it.'

'Then indulge in it, Colonel. The gentleman sharing the suite with you at the Grand Hotel of the Baths and of Serbia is not the King of Mittenstein-Hoffnung – true or false?'

'I have no comment to make on that subject.'

'Would it surprise you to know that he's dead?'

'Surprise me? No, not particularly. Poor feller.'

'And we have evidence to show that the body is not that of His Majesty.'

'In which case, the matter speaks for itself.'

'So who was the man you shared the suite with?'

'No reason why you shouldn't know now – a double.'

'Planted with you by the king.'

'Indeed.'

'So the king went through his usual motions of pretending to be at Baden-Baden and then coming here, except that he planted a double here.'

'You could put it like that.'

'Was the double an official double?'

'A distant cousin of his who picked up a little money by doubling for him on those occasions when there seemed danger of assassination.'

'As the double was assassinated, it looks as if it was one of those occasions.'

'It does rather, yes. Where did it happen?'

'On the beach.'

'When?'

'Last Monday.'

'But I saw him on the beach on Wednesday afternoon – with a lot of policemen.'

'Oh, that wasn't him. That was his double.'

'You mean, the double had a double?'

'Yes.'

'Who organized that?'

'We did.'

'Confusing.'

'He was assassinated too. Where's the real king?'

'I don't know.'

'Is that honest, Colonel?'

'Absolutely. I know where he ought to be, but he's not there.'

'Will you tell me where he ought to be?'

'No, because that's absolutely top secret.'

'Are you worried because he isn't where he ought to be?'

'Very.'

'It's nice to have met you, Colonel.'

'Where are you off to?'

'Back to Paris. My department is always glad to co-operate when a king has been murdered, but not when it happens to a double; that's a routine police job.'

'But the king has disappeared. Isn't it your department's job to find him?'

'If we're asked to, but we should have to know first where he's supposed to be.'

'I'll have to get permission to tell you that.'

'Then I suggest you do so.'

127

'It'll take time. I'll tell you tomorrow. I wonder who killed the double.'

'And the double's double.'

'Baffling, isn't it. Here come your oysters.'

If the real king was to be assassinated, thought Picard, it was a pity it hadn't happened at the time when Gibeau and the double were lying side by side in the fish market cellar: to have seen the three matching corpses together would have been a most unusual and rewarding sight.

As soon as the train arrived, Grunwald disinterred Body A from the load of chemical fertilizer, conveyed it to the fish market on the handcart, and manhandled it down into the cellar. He laid it tidily on the table, but did little towards cleaning it up, apart from pouring a bucket of water over it and rubbing it rather gingerly and ineffectually with a piece of brown paper: there were limits, he considered, to his versatility.

When he came up the stairs, he saw Picard waiting for him in the street outside.

'I have another job for you,' said Picard.

'I've got to get the key of the cellar back to the Bonpain.'

'I'll take it.'

'Just as you like. You know, I've just thought of something. The undertaker will be going down there to fetch what he thinks is Gibeau's body –'

'Yes.'

'And he'll expect to see two bodies there.'

'And so he shall, Grunwald, so he shall.'

'I don't understand you.'

'Grunwald, you have a task to perform which may not be altogether to your liking.'

Grunwald felt a cold, hard knot form in his stomach. 'What do I do?'

'First of all, you lock yourself inside the cellar gate, then hand me the key through the bars.'

'Then what?'

'You go down the steps, Grunwald, and remove your clothing.'

'All of it?'

'Certainly – which you will hide in a fish basket. You will then place yourself on the table, alongside the corpse, covering yourself with a sheet.'

'Why?'

'So that the undertaker, going down to take the corpse, will see the two corpses which he will expect to see,' explained Picard, patiently.

'Suppose he tries to take me?'

'A good point, Grunwald, and one I've attended to. Take these two luggage labels. You must uncover one of the corpse's feet, to which you will tie one of the labels on which you will have written, in large letters, "INSPECTOR GIBEAU".'

'But it won't be Inspector Gibeau.'

'Don't quibble, Grunwald. You will then attach the other label, bearing the words "UNKNOWN MALE BODY", to one of your own feet.'

'I haven't got a sheet,' said Grunwald, throwing every possible obstacle in the way.

'I have one here for you.' Picard took a neat parcel from under his arm. 'Bring it back to the hotel afterwards, it belongs on your bed.'

'Oh, look, really – '

'It's for France, Grunwald.'

Tuesday 16 September

The next day was to be a heavy one for Father Gérard. First, there was to be the funeral of Inspector Gibeau, which had been arranged for fairly early in the morning, because it was the feast day of St Evian of the Running Sores, which is traditionally celebrated by a procession through the streets, followed by a service of thanksgiving, followed by various secular festivities.

As he shaved and dressed himself, pausing from time to time to take a fortifying sip of cognac, the good father reviewed in his mind the origins of the day of rejoicing. Back in the thirteenth century, there had been a miracle: on the very day on which the wicked and licentious English had taken possession of the town, the wooden statue of the saint, which was venerated in the church, was observed to have real running sores. Naturally, thousands of the faithful had come from miles around to witness this curiously patriotic manifestation of the Holy Spirit. Perturbed by the number of people flooding into the town, the English commander, Sir Edward Tolworth, had ordered that the statue should be taken out into the market square and burned – and there were those among the crowd who had testified that the smoke from the fire had assumed the shape of the Holy Grail, although how the observers could have known the shape of the Grail was never explained. When the occupying English forces were eventually driven out of the town, a new wooden statue of St Evian was carved but, alas, no matter how severe the misfortune which hit the populace, there was no sign of the sores running.

Came the Revolution, and that statue, in its turn, was burned, this time by the vandalous followers of Robespierre. With the Restoration, a third statue was carved, and this was the one which would be carried round the streets today. It was poorly sculpted but, at a whim of the craftsman, under the wooden vestments there was a swelling shape where the trunk forks, which put speculative ideas into the head of many a white-clad virgin walking in procession.

When one drinks as much cognac as Father Gérard, it is difficult to gauge exactly the effect each succeeding glass will have, and the glass taken in the vestry before setting out on foot for the cemetery with the mourners, was noticed to have produced a swaying effect as he walked.

At the graveside, Picard found himself standing next to Bonpain, and he observed a tear of compassion slowly rolling down the commissaire's cheek. Seeking to comfort him, he leaned over and whispered into his ear, 'Don't worry, it's not Gibeau.'

Startled, Bonpain turned and asked, 'Who is it then?'

'The other one.'

'His Majesty?'

'A distant cousin of His Majesty's.'

'I don't understand.'

'It's a complicated story; I'll tell you afterwards.' Picard was happy to notice that his comforting words had had a good effect, because he saw no more tears on Bonpain's cheeks.

The culmination of the burial was to be the volley fired into the air by six of Gibeau's comrades, which was to be the cue for the grave-diggers to start throwing earth on the coffin. *Sergent de Ville* Maupas was the one who had been entrusted with the task of loading the rifles with blank ammunition, and he was perturbed to see that the shot fired by the man on the extreme left of the line downed a passing rook.

This phenomenon impressed Father Gérard so much that he leaned forward to watch the fall of the unfortunate bird, and this, in the father's condition, was an ill-advised thing to do, as he overbalanced and fell into the grave, landing flat on top of the coffin. The grave-diggers, having been given their cue, had turned to obtain shovel-fuls of earth, and there was no time to stop them scattering these over the recumbent priest.

Fortunately, it was a dry day, and Father Gérard was easily dusted down. It was also fortunate that, as the funeral was being paid for out of police funds, orders had been given to the undertakers to keep costs down as much as posible, so the grave was no deeper than the statutory minimum.

The funeral party then dispersed, most of them to nearby cafés, although Gibeau's sisters went straight to the railway station, very sour-faced and having seen nothing funny in Father Gérard's fall from grace.

Picard took Bonpain to the Café des Colonnes, where he kept his promise by telling him as much as he thought advisable of what had been going on in the background. He also invited him to assist at the interrogation of Lord Sherrington that afternoon. He had heard no more from Paris and, as he had no further body to send to Mittenstein-Hoffnung, decided to do nothing for the time being.

Grunwald did not attend the funeral, mainly because nobody had invited him. He had had a very miserable time the previous day, pretending to be a corpse, and Picard had forgotten to release him from the cellar until quite late in the evening.

He went and sat on the goods-yard fence and considered a moral problem. When he had asked Picard for instructions as to what to do with the chemical fertilizer, the answer had been, 'Do anything you like with it, it's all yours.' Did that mean that he was entitled to sell it and pocket the profits? Or did honesty demand that he should hand over the proceeds to the cashier of the department? Because, after all, the man in Mittenstein-Hoffnung presumably had bought it on his expense account.

He reminded himself that he had overcome his scruples in agreeing to accept a quarter share of the difference in the wholesale price between salted cod for selling and salted cod for eating, but, on that occasion, he had quieted his conscience by telling himself he was merely conforming to what was obviously one of the customs of the trade. The present case was different.

Anyway, the first step was to sell the stuff. He shelved the moral issue, got down from the fence, and set off for the café kept by the short, thick man with the permanent dewdrop.

There was a small room on the top floor of the commissariat which was known as the interrogation room. It was bare and cheerless, but it was away from such distractions as the telephone, and its isolated position meant that the shouting of an interrogator or the cries of protest, or possibly pain, of the interrogated would disturb nobody.

Sergent de Ville Maupas had received orders to take Lord Sherrington up there at two o'clock, at which hour Picard anticipated being back from luncheon. Despite the sparse comfort of the cell in which he had spent the night, His Lordship managed to look his usual impeccable self, an impression accentuated by the fact that he was wearing white tie and tails, because Grunwald had refused to allow him time to choose more suitable clothes. He sat, seemingly relaxed and at ease, on a plain wooden chair, while Maupas prowled restlessly round the room, looking at his watch. The *sergent de ville* was now supposed to be off duty, and he had a rendezvous with the lady at the beach toys shop for a little amorous dalliance in the back room before she went home to her husband.

From outside in the passage came a series of thumps as *Sergent de Ville* Petel, who would have been the commissariat librarian if there had been a library, rearranged the dozen or so law books plus the hundreds of back numbers of *The Police Illustrated* and *The Police Journal*, which gathered dust on some rickety shelves.

Maupas opened the door and went out. 'Are you going to be here for a while, Petel?'

'About half an hour, while I sort this stuff out.'

'I've got a prisoner in here, waiting for interrogation.'

'Oh? Who by?'

'The man from Paris – what ever his name is. He was supposed to be here at two o'clock, and he's late. Be a pal and keep an eye on the prisoner for me, because I'm supposed to be off duty. We're three floors up and he can't get out except by this door.'

'Has it got a lock?'

'Yes, of course it has. If I lock the door and you keep an eye on him from out here, nobody can complain he's not being guarded, can they?'

'Suppose what ever his name is isn't back when I've finished?'

'Then you put the prisoner back in the cells. Go on, I'll do as much for you one day.'

'All right then.'

Maupas went back into the room. 'You behave yourself. I'm going off now, but there's a colleague of mine out in the passage, so it's no good you starting anything.'

He had hardly locked the door before Sherry was out of the window. It was not an easy climb down; the room was at the back of the building, looking on to a side street, and there was little decoration breaking the sheer wall. An added complication was the necessity to avoid windows. Luckily, it was an old building and the brickwork badly needed re-pointing, so there were narrow finger and toe holds in the brickwork, and, for part of the way, some well-established ivy.

There were few passers-by in the street below, and none looked up. From a window in a house opposite, a small girl of about two watched his progress with solemn interest, but she was more concerned with an orange she was eating. When he eventually dropped to the pavement, a man wheeling a barrow said, 'Cor, you give me a start, you did. Where did you come from?'

'We're making a film,' said Sherry.

'Where's the camera then?'

'Up there.' He pointed to the roof of the house opposite. 'You'll be in it too. You were very good.' He walked away along the street.

He realized that he was not going to get back to his hotel unobserved, because there are few who promenade in evening clothes at two-thirty on a summer afternoon; in fact, at that moment he was being given curious looks by a waiter at the Café Momus, which he was passing. He could not even take a taxi, because the police had impounded all his money.

In the near distance, there was a shot. Good God! were they shooting at him now? Then he realized that the shot probably heralded the start of one of the races forming part of the festivities which traditionally followed the religious celebrations. Yes, he was right, for here came the runners – or rather the walkers, because it was the waiters' race. There was a field of twenty-seven, all in their professional evening clothes and each carrying a tray on which was a glass and a bottle of a well-known brand of aperitif, the proprietors of which had presented a challenge cup and a prize of five hundred francs.

The waiter at the Café Momus had put his tray down on a terrace table while he shouted encouragement to a colleague who was competing.

'Look,' shouted Sherry, 'that poor chap has fainted.' The waiter turned to look, and Sherry snatched up the tray and joined the race, lying twenty-eighth but making good progress because he hadn't a bottle and glass to balance.

He found himself walking beside Jules Peyronnet, the non-swimming life guard who doubled as waiter at Le Florida.

'Where's your bottle?'

'It fell off.'

'You're disqualified then; you'll have to retire.'

'I'm enjoying the walk,' said Sherry. 'How long is the course?'

'Six kilometres.'

134

'Jesus!' said Sherry.

'I've seen you before, but I can't place you,' said Peyronnet. 'Where do you work?'

'The Café Momus.'

'What's happened to Henri then?'

'He had a miscarriage,' said Sherry.

By now, the race was proceeding down the Rue Thiers and approaching the Grand Hotel of the Baths and of Serbia, so Sherry peeled off, pressing his tray into the hands of a passing old lady, who was delighted because it was just what her daughter-in-law wanted. He ran up the alley to the staff entrance and mounted the back stairs.

'I think we'd better leave,' he said, as he entered the suite he shared with his cousin.

'Did they let you go?' asked Anthony.

'No, I left.'

'We don't stand much chance of getting away in daylight.'

'We won't try; we'll wait until dark.'

'Where do we wait?'

'Here's as good as anywhere.'

'In this suite?'

'No, you idiot. While I change, go and hide the Lanchester.'

'Not easy. Where's the best place?'

'The best place is usually the most obvious one.' He pondered for a moment. 'The proprietor of that car showroom near the Opera House was admiring it the other day. Go and ask him if he'd like to put it in his shop window. Tell him we shan't be using it for a day or two and it might mean he'll get an order for one.'

'What do we do with all our luggage?'

'Ditch it.'

'What about my suits?'

'The suit they'd give you in jail is really horrid.'

The Hon. Anthony left at once.

Even the oldest inhabitant of the commissariat had never seen the commissaire in such a rage.

Bonpain and Picard had entered the interrogation room just two minutes after Sherry had left it. Leaning out of the open window, Picard had seen the fresh scratches on the brickwork, which told him all he needed to know. They tore downstairs and interviewed the man with the barrow.

'Did you see a man come down this wall?' shouted Bonpain.

'Yes, he's in a film,' said the old man. 'He said I was in it and I was very good. He said the camera's up there.' He pointed to the child who was sucking the orange in the house opposite. 'All dressed up, he was.'

Bonpain thought quickly. He had been told that Sherry was in evening clothes and, on ordinary form, should not be difficult to pick up, but he was coming to the conclusion that Sherry was the kind of man to whom ordinary form did not apply.

There was a distant crack.

'A shot!' said Picard.

Bonpain glanced at his watch. 'It's just the start of the waiters' race,' he said.

In his turn, Picard thought quickly. 'Don't you see? That's how the bastard is going to get through the town. All the waiters will be in evening clothes, so he'll join in.'

'He won't have a tray,' said Bonpain.

'He'll steal a tray.'

'Yes, he probably would.' The commissaire turned to Lautier. 'I want all the competitors in the waiters' race arrested. At once – before they finish the course.'

Nearing the end of their gruelling six-kilometre course, the field of the race was strung out, with an unpopular Roumanian from the Café of the Abattoir in the lead and Jules Peyronnet lying a dogged third. They were just turning the corner by Madame Zizi's when a posse of police jumped from their bicycles and arrested them one by one.

Twenty-seven panting waiters were herded into a cul-de-sac behind a soapworks and checked and double-checked. The Roumanian announced that he would complain to his consulate and that it was typical of French sportsmanship that the race should be interrupted when he was winning. The other competitors took the matter more philosophically and opened their bottles.

The only useful information came from Peyronnet. 'There was this chap beside me without a bottle, and his face was vaguely familiar. "Where are you from?" I said, and he said "From the Café Momus" and I said, "Has Henri left then?" and I knew he wouldn't have, because he's sleeping with the proprietor's wife and getting special treatment, and then this chap peeled off.'

'Whereabouts were you when he peeled off?' asked Picard, who had arrived on the scene with Bonpain.

'It was just as we were passing the Grand Hotel of the Baths and of Serbia.'

'I knew it!' exclaimed Picard. 'Tell me, Monsieur Peyronnet, you thought you'd seen this man before; could it have been at the bathing establishment? Could it have been on the morning of the first murder?'

Peyronnet snapped his fingers. 'Yes,' he said, 'that's where I'd seen him. It was that morning. I showed him into a cabin on the men's side.'

'And he could have climbed over the trellis fence while you were in the end cabin with Anne-Marie,' accused Bonpain, sternly.

Peyronnet hung his head.

'To the Grand Hotel of the Baths and of Serbia, and quickly,' said Picard, taking Bonpain by the arm.

'He'll have gone by now,' said Bonpain.

'Perhaps – perhaps not. Have your men look for the Lanchester.'

Picard and Bonpain departed for the hotel in a police car driven by an elderly *sergent de ville* who was very short sighted but trying to disguise the fact so that he could work out his full time; as a result, he drove very slowly and very dangerously. When they arrived there was no sign of the two Englishmen.

'I'll swear they won't get far,' said Bonpain. 'Every road is being watched, and it won't take us long to pick up the car.'

'Search their rooms, Bonpain. Check every item of clothing and every possession; find out every single thing you can about them. Where the hell's Grunwald? Why isn't he helping?' He made for the door.

'Where are you going?'

'I'm going to see someone who, I hope, will give us considerable elucidation.' Picard went to the room of Colonel Withers, who was taking a rejuvenating dish of apricots.

'I hope, Colonel, that you can now tell me all you know, for the sake of the real king and for the sake of peace in Europe.'

'I'm glad to say I have permission to do so. Who won the waiters' race?'

'We had to stop it.'

'A pity. I rather fancied the chances of that very tall waiter in the restaurant. In fact, I had twenty francs on him. Did you notice how he was doing?'

'He was nowhere.'

'Splendid, I saved my money. Sit down. May I offer you a glass of something?'

'No, thank you. May we get down to business?'

'Right. Taking things in their proper sequence, I've been here with His Majesty on a number of his jaunts, at which times he has always arranged an alibi at Baden-Baden. You know all that.'

'Yes, Colonel.'

'Incidentally, I hear that the manager of the hotel at Baden-Baden fell down his own stairs and broke his neck.'

'Very unfortunate.'

'I suppose your people arranged that.'

'I fear so.'

'This time, His Majesty was laying a doubly confusing trail by setting-up his usual alibi at Baden-Baden and then putting his double in here with me.'

'And it was the double who was stabbed on the first occasion at the bathing establishment.'

'Yes. I never took to the fellow.'

'Was he – er – homosexual?'

'Quite astonishingly. The real king will never be able to come back here again : the page boys would protest.'

'At which point was the changeover made between the king and the double?'

'It was made here. The king arrived first, and he spoke to the manager and the barman and all the people in the hotel who knew him, and that evening the double arrived in a hired car. He got out of the car at that badly-lit part of the promenade just beyond the statue of Edeodat Thion, which is no work of art, and His Majesty got in.'

'And where was His Majesty bound for?'

'Paris.'

'Why?'

'This is the secret bit, old boy. Germany wants war, and at the first excuse they'll set Europe alight. Mind you, they're bloody crazy because you and us and the Russians will see them off in no time, but the Kaiser won't be told what's best for him.'

'Is this a matter of cauxite?'

'You've hit it. Mittenstein-Hoffnung's on our side; I mean, damn it, HM went to Harrow. He set off for Paris to negotiate a deal whereby the Allies can have all the cauxite they need in exchange for the defence of the sovereignty of Mittenstein-Hoffnung. Now, if anyone on the other side had got wind of this, there's a very good reason for rubbing out His Majesty before he could sign the treaty.'

'And he hasn't got to Paris.'

'No, he's disappeared. Apart from being very worrying, it's also embarrassing, because Lloyd George is waiting there, and Asquith, and Poincaré, and a couple of Russian grand dukes.'

'So it's probable that the people we're looking for are Germans, or mercenaries working for the Germans.'

'They're not very bright, whoever they are, because they've killed two wrong 'uns.'

'Without going into details, I'll have to pass some of this on.'

'That's understood, but you are to say nothing about the diplomatic stuff. All you know is that HM was bound for Paris to make a trade deal which could have been detrimental to German industrial interests. You can say it's possible that those interests would try to stop the deal, perhaps going to the extent of hiring professional assassins.'

'Understood, Colonel. Thank you.'

'I'll tell you, it's put me right off; I'm no good to any woman when I'm worried.'

On the promenade, to his joy, Picard encountered Ernestine. Having heard nothing, he had resigned himself to the thought that she had already left the town. She was wearing a peach-coloured silk dress, a summery hat decorated with cornflowers and daisies, and she carried a cream sunshade.

'Peaches and cream,' said Picard. 'It's a long time since we met.'

'Very true, darling; you've been terribly neglectful.'

'Perhaps I didn't want to interfere with your intensive social life.' Picard failed to hide the tinge of bitterness in his voice.

'Was I supposed to sit at home with my sewing? I was teaching you a lesson.'

'I'd made it clear that I had a lot of work to do.'

'Am I going to see anything of you today? Cécile sings her first performance of Carmen tonight, and I'm quite free. Would you like to come with me?'

'My love, I'm afraid – '

'All right, you don't have to tell me, but you see what I mean – and I was staying on in this town especially for your benefit.'

'At least it's better than Etaples.'

'I could have had two days in Paris.'

'I'm sorry, darling.'

'Whatever happens, I have to leave tomorrow.' She looked at him with her head on one side, and said, 'I always knew you were a jealous devil, but you're carrying it a bit far, aren't you?'

'What do you mean?'

'Anthony tells me that you've arrested Sherry.'

'Everyone gets arrested here; you've been arrested twice yourself.' Anxiously, he asked, 'You haven't seen either of them within the last hour or two, have you?'

'My sweet, I've only just got up, and I promise you neither of them has been in my bedroom.'

'I'm relieved to hear it.'

'Darling, I have very high standards.'

'They're both very well connected.'

'That's not what I meant, and you know it. So you're not coming to Carmen?'

'I'll try – but I doubt it.'

'The management has given me a box, so I'll keep a seat for you, in case.' She kissed him sensuously on the lips. 'If you get any time off during the rest of the day, I'll be in my room.'

Picard walked swiftly to the commissariat. He sat in Bonpain's office while the commissaire was busy on the telephone, issuing orders for the scouring of the countryside for the two Englishmen. When he paused for breath, Picard told him as much as Withers had authorized that he should be told.

'It gives us some background, at any rate,' said Bonpain. 'I still think the evidence against Sherrington is thin : all we've got against him is that he likes to climb up buildings, and that he sings a song that anyone else might sing.'

'He escaped from arrest, didn't he?'

'I don't blame him for that. Any spirited lad would do the same.'

'And they've disappeared, leaving all their belongings behind.'

'They may have gone for a ride in the country.'

'Did you find anything among their possessions?'

'Nothing in the least suspicious. The clothes and luggage are English, and there are no personal papers or effects.'

'I find that suspicious in itself. You know, it's always possible someone else is involved – someone older, directing their operations. Can you give me a man to help me go through the files of all the foreigners in the town?'

'I can give you Verdi.'

'Good.'

'Why don't you work up in the interrogation room? You'll be quieter there.'

Picard carried the armful of files upstairs. In a few moments, Verdi joined him, saluting smartly.

'Sit down, Verdi, I want your help.'

'With pleasure, Monsieur.'

'Incidentally, I enjoyed your piano playing the other evening.'

'It's a pastime, but I have little talent.'

'I wish I had half of it. Now listen, we're going through these files, and I want to know if anyone has been to Mittenstein-Hoffnung, which is unlikely, or is German, or has German interests.'

They set to work. Vaquin and his men had done a thorough job; the questioning had been intelligently done, and statements had been checked against passport entries. In view of the general anti-German feeling, there were very few Teutonic visitors, and those were nearly all business representatives.

'I know this one,' said Verdi, displaying a file. 'He sells machinery, and for a German he's not a bad fellow. He's the one I played German tunes for, the other evening.' He paused. 'I've just remembered something.'

'Well?'

'I played German tunes for the German visitor, and he was kind enough to applaud me and he sent me a bottle of wine – '

'Yes, I saw that.'

' – and I played English tunes for the two young Englishmen. Now, I'm always interested to watch the reaction of my audience, and it struck me that the Englishmen were nodding their heads and tapping their feet much more to the German tunes than they were to the English tunes.'

Picard jumped to his feet, upsetting the pile of files. 'Bless you, Verdi,' he said. 'Come and tell that to the commissaire.'

Bonpain listened to Verdi's story, and then turned to Picard with

141

a bewildered look. 'I've been a policeman for thirty years,' he said, 'and never before have I been given a musical clue. Now you give me two of them.'

'One clue could be circumstantial, Bonpain, but not two.'

'All right, so those two Englishmen are the villains and we have to get them – but we're trying to do that already. Why can't we find that Lanchester?' He picked up the telephone.

If the commissaire only knew, his men had been walking past it for hours: in the car dealer's window, it was in the most prominent site in the town.

Sherry and Anthony were not far away, either. They had climbed on to the roof of the hotel and were installed between a chimney stack and the mansard of one of the attic rooms in which the staff slept in crowded conditions. Each of the cousins in turn took a spell of lying flat and peering over the coping stone, to watch who went in and out of the main entrance, while the other played patience.

Cécile pulled her mink wrap about her ears, and looked across the room at the man in her bed. 'I never thought I'd ever be going to the Opera House in mink,' she said. 'I'm so glad Ernestine is staying an extra day or two; I can't wait to see her face.'

'You're the sort of girl who ought to drip with diamonds,' said the man.

'Well, I'm willing, if you are.'

'Give me time, my love. We haven't known each other long.'

'Promise me you won't be late for the performance.'

'I promise. I wish you hadn't put me in a box.'

'Where else should you sit, except in a box?'

'But you know the place is a *théâtre à femmes*. A lot of the girls know me, and they might call out.'

'You shouldn't have such a disreputable past.' She went to the bed and gave him a lingering kiss. 'See you later, Coco,' she said.

Cécile's departure from the hotel was watched from the roof. 'He'll be on his own now,' said Anthony.

'It's still too light to go down. We took a chance climbing up here in daylight; we ought not to take another. He won't leave until the last minute.'

'I hope you're right, Sherry.'

'I've been right all the time so far.'

'Not all the time. Remember our two boss shots.'

'Let's call them sighters.'

'I still think it's clever of you, finding out where he is.'

'It was just a stroke of luck. Quite by chance, we take a couple of opera singers out to supper in the country and on the way back one of them starts to sing – not an aria from *Carmen*, or *Lakmé*, or *Manon*, but the Mittenstein-Hoffnung national anthem. There had to be a reason.'

'I'd never have recognized the bloody tune.'

'Let's face it, Anthony, you're not really musical.'

Ernestine pulled her rabbit-skin cape about her ears and looked across the room at the man in her bed. 'I do appreciate your visit, Chanteloup darling, brief though it's been, and I do wish you'd take me to the opera.'

'I'm sorry, my love, but the case that I'm working on is just at its climax.'

'It can't be all that important. What does it matter if you arrest somebody today or tomorrow?'

'Can I trust you not to breathe a word if I tell you about it?' Now that certain details had, to some extent, been released, there seemed no reason for not letting Ernestine know what important matters he dealt with.

'You can tell me if you like; I won't pass it on. Why should I?'

'The two murders – the ones you were suspected of . . .'

'Aren't I suspected of them any more?'

'No, my love.'

'It'd be nice if somebody told me. I'd got quite used to the feel of handcuffs.'

'Those two men were murdered because the killers mistook them for the King of Mittenstein-Hoffnung.'

'Oh, so that's what he looks like.'

'We're now worried that the killers might be on the trail of the real King of Mittenstein-Hoffnung.'

'Who are the murderers?'

'We're pretty sure it's your friends Sherrington and Anthony.'

'Go on!'

'But they've disappeared.'

'You'd better find them then.'

'That's what we're trying to do.'

'I hope the king's being well protected.'

'He would be, if we knew where he was.'

'You don't know where he is?'

'No.'

'Well, I can tell you that.'

'What?' Picard sprang out of bed. 'Where?'

'You look disgusting like that.'

'Where?'

'In Cécile's bed.'

'Cécile's bed? Since when?'

'Days and days. She picked him up on the promenade as he was getting into a car one evening. She says she dropped her parasol and he stooped to retrieve it. When she discovered he was a king, she was delighted: it was one in the eye for me, because I've only got a minister.'

'The king was supposed to be going to Paris.'

'He didn't like the idea of Paris; he preferred the idea of Cécile.'

'He's been in her room all the time?'

'I suppose so. He'll have to come out to go to the opera.'

'What's the number of Cécile's room? Here, you'd better come with me.'

'Not like that, darling. Put some clothes on.'

'Damn it to hell!' said Anthony, as he watched the king walk out of the hotel.

'It can't be helped,' said Sherry. 'We were quite right to be sensible and wait for dusk. We weren't to know he would leave early.'

'It would have been so easy to kill him in the bedroom.'

'It'll probably be even easier to kill him in the Opera House.'

'It'll be more difficult to get away.'

'Not necessarily. Come on, it's dark enough now. Let's go in.'

'How do we get out of the hotel?'

'The staff entrance, of course. You don't think they keep track of all the casual help they hire to wash-up. I'm afraid you'll have to ruffle your hair.'

His Majesty strolled slowly along the promenade. He was wearing his white tie and tails, which Cécile had collected from his suite while Colonel Withers was out, and an order or two graced his left breast.

The moonlight flashed across the dark water on which rode the gleaming and expensive yachts of rich members of international society. It was the beautiful, constant and secure world to which His Majesty was accustomed. He stopped and looked at his watch, designed for him by Fabergé. He knew it was early, but hadn't realized how early, and he certainly didn't want to sit in the auditorium before the performance started, with all those vulgar girls waving, or even calling, to him. He selected a deck chair under a street lamp, and sat down for a few minutes. He lay back, half closing his eyes.

Jules Peyronnet was walking home; it had been a long, tiring day. As he came to the street lamp, he glanced at the figure in the deck chair. His blood froze. He saw the half-closed eyes, the plump face, the small moustache.

It was the third of them! It must be an omen! He fell in a gentle faint.

'*Merde!*' said Picard, as he surveyed Cécile's empty room.

'Don't worry, you're bound to find him at the Opera House,' said Ernestine.

'I'll telephone the comissariat. I'll have the building surrounded.'

'And frighten off Sherry and Anthony? I thought you wanted to catch them.'

'I suppose you're right; I hadn't thought of that.'

'You see how much you need me, darling.'

'But they'll be after the king. We've got to protect him.'

'I'm quite sure we'll be able to look after the old sod between us. We'd better hurry, they'll be ringing up in a few minutes – and I must say I'm not accustomed to going to the opera with a gentleman who isn't in evening clothes.'

A peculiarity of the Opera House was that its ornate entrance was in a squalid side street, while the back of the building faced the promenade and the sea. Possibly the architect's idea was that opera-going ladies would prefer a few steps amid squalor rather than have their skirts blown over their heads by the sea breezes.

By using a series of drainpipes, Sherry and Anthony had no difficulty in scaling the rear elevation; in fact, Sherry had done so before, to plant a chamber pot. As they shinned up past each dressing-room, they heard the scales, gurgles and throat clearings of the singers who were preparing for the performance. Near the top of the building, they found a grimy, unlatched window, which opened at a touch. They found themselves in a strange, high world of ropes and pulleys and sandbags and rolled-up backcloths. Aided by light coming up from the stage, they made their way along a narrow iron catwalk until they came to a ladder bolted to the wall. They went down six or seven metres until they came to another catwalk, much bigger and wider.

A man in blue overalls moved past them, carrying a piece of lighting equipment. 'Who are you?' he asked belligerently.

Sherry rose to the occasion. 'The boss says you're to get the spotlight on Carmen immediately at her first entrance; he says you were a bit slow at rehearsal.'

He and Anthony went on their way, leaving the electrician lifting his cap to scratch his head. What was Blanc up to? Time and money were never wasted on lighting rehearsals; they just did the best they could when they came to it.

Reaching the stage, the two intruders justified their presence by addressing the chorus. Sherry told the soldiers that the boss said they were to put their shoulders back and look much more military, while Anthony told the girls from the cigarette factory that they were to show much more leg.

The orchestra were now tuning up and the cast were taking their places. Sherry and Anthony found their way below the stage and through a small, low door into the orchestra pit. The prompter, a very old man with a permanent cough caused by the dust kicked up by decades of singers, was making his way into his box. The house lights went down, and Monsieur Rochebrun appeared on the podium to a scattering of applause.

'You go that way, I'll go this,' Sherry whispered to Anthony. 'As soon as we see where he's sitting, the one who's nearest to him fires.' He turned left among the musicians, pushing his way between two double bassists. 'I'm looking for an electrical fault,' he explained. At the other end of the pit, Anthony was telling a bewildered bassoonist not to blow too hard during the Toreador's Song in case he blew the bends out of his instrument.

Monsieur Rochebrun tapped his music stand, gave a perfunctory wave of his baton and brought the orchestra in on the downbeat.

His Majesty, still fearful of catcalls from his female acquaintances, did not go into his box during the orchestral prelude, nor during the opening scene between the soldiers and Micaela; it was only when he heard Carmen's entrance music and the chorus singing 'Here she is! Here's Carmencita!' that he opened the door and stepped in, to be instantly visible in the light spilling out from the stage.

Not only Sherry and Anthony were watching for him, but also Ernestine and Picard, who were in a stage box on the other side. They saw the king at the same time that they saw Sherry and Anthony rise up from among the seated musicians, both with revolvers in their hands. Picard jumped down into the pit and fought his way among the brass players to reach Sherry, who turned and fired at him, missing him completely but taking the wig off a trombone player. Ernestine, throwing off her rabbit-skin cape, had jumped on to the stage and was running along the footlights. The audience, recognizing her as an old favourite, gave her unexpected appearance a cheer. She reached the centre of the stage just as Cécile received her cue to sing her first words, 'When shall I love you?', but Ernestine drowned her by cupping her two hands to her mouth and shouting 'DUCK, Your Majesty!' Warned since childhood that every monarch should be ready to duck immediately on every public occasion, the king did as he was advised, and Anthony's shot passed harmlessly over his head.

Cécile, livid with rage at having her rival run in front of her just as she was making her entrance, took a run and kicked Ernestine so hard on the bottom that she was projected over the footlights and into the orchestra pit. One way and another, there was a lot going on in the orchestra pit.

Sherry and Anthony climbed over the rail into the auditorium, each running up a side aisle, with Picard pursuing Sherry, whose gun had been snatched from him by a horn player, who was not in the least brave but just angry because it had gone off in his ear.

Dashing through the foyer, Sherry had a comfortable lead, with Anthony in second place only a metre or two in front of Picard. As they ran down the steps and on to the pavement, Picard reached out and grabbed Anthony by the arm. Anthony twisted free but both men lost their balance and fell, rolling on the ground, the gun flying from Anthony's hand. He didn't pause to pick it up but aimed a kick at Picard's head which caught him on the cheekbone and put him down again.

Sherry was making for the car saleroom. On their way to the

theatre, the two men had placed a few bricks in a strategic position, and Sherry picked one up and hurled it through the plate glass window. Anthony climbed through the hole and began to wind up the starting handle of the Lanchester, while Sherry cleared jagged fragments of glass from the frame of the window.

The engine spluttered and then roared. Anthony sprang into the driver's seat and drove the car through the cleared space in the window. Sherry jumped into the passenger seat of the open car as it went by, unfortunately landing on some broken pieces of glass which had fallen on to the seat.

Whistles were sounding from the Opera House behind them. Ahead, the promenade was deserted, except for a morose and solitary figure. It was Grunwald, who was on his way to post a letter of resignation.

By calling, from time to time, at the commissariat, he had kept in touch with what was going on, but Picard had not sought his assistance and, indeed, during the whole investigation had entrusted him only with the most menial tasks. On reflection, he supposed he could hardly blame him because, after all, it was he, Grunwald, who had let the presumed king be killed in the first place, and then turned up drunk for the first salted cod loading.

He felt an abject sense of failure, intensified by a total lack of success in selling the chemical fertilizer: a failing due as much to circumstance as to his own inability – he had learnt from those he had approached that, since it was an agricultural area, there was plenty of honest manure about and why should anybody want to bother with this new-fangled rubbish? To add to his miseries, he was sure he had a cold coming on, caught no doubt from the hours he had spent naked in the cellar of the fish market. No, there was no doubt he had been a liability in every phase of the case. In the morning, he would take the first train to Paris and seek some less demanding form of employment, perhaps in the clothing trade, where he had family contacts.

He turned and saw the Lanchester racing towards him, with Picard dazedly and doggedly pounding in pursuit. Almost as if by instinct, Grunwald stepped in front of the car.

'Stop!' he shouted.

Anthony, although ready to assassinate a king, had a conscience so far as killing a pedestrian was concerned, and he swung the wheel hard over. The car skidded and almost stalled. In that moment,

Grunwald leapt, landing on top of Sherry, who screamed as the glass fragments did their fell work. The car careened across the promenade, smashed through the railings on to the beach, and overturned in the soft sand.

Picard and several *sergents de ville* were on top of Sherry and Anthony before they could move. Grunwald, lying in the sand where he had been hurled, was gazing in fascination at one of the Lanchester's wheels, which had hit a rock and buckled. Broken wire spokes stuck out like the spines of a half-bald porcupine.

'Are you all right, Grunwald?' called Picard, with unexpected solicitude.

'Look!' Grunwald was pointing a shaking finger at the wheel. 'I'll bet one of those spokes was the first murder weapon.'

There was a large and cheerful party at the Café des Colonnes after the performance, which had continued uninterrupted despite the extra excitements to which the audience had been treated. His Majesty sat at the head of the table, of course, and had been generously bestowing Orders of the Golden Turkey, First Class. Ernestine sat on his right, bravely ignoring a very bruised bottom, while Cécile, on his left, was magnanimous in her forgiveness for the ruining of her first entrance. Next to her sat Grunwald, now acclaimed as a hero and with no thought at all of posting his letter of resignation. On the other side of Ernestine sat Picard, who had a strip of sticking plaster on his cheek: as he would surely have some leave due to him at the successful conclusion of the case, he was planning to go with her to Étaples, where they could spend a blissful ten days together before she returned to the embraces of the Minister of Justice. Bonpain, just back from the commissariat, was beaming, and so was Colonel Withers, who was starting his third dozen oysters. Inspector Verdi, by special request, was at the piano.

'There's no doubt about it,' said Withers, 'both the buggers are German.'

'They admitted that,' said Bonpain, 'after we exerted a little pressure – and Monsieur Grunwald was right about one of the wheel spokes having been used for the first murder.'

Grunwald flushed with pleasure.

'Another thing,' said Withers. 'I'll bet they were never at Cambridge.'

'No, they weren't; they read English at Heidelberg. Incidentally, I

149

still don't know what all that nonsense of putting chamber pots on roofs was all about.'

'They were overacting,' explained Withers. 'They thought it was the sort of thing that Cambridge men do. It is, too – or it was in my day.'

'They aren't a very bright couple,' said Picard. 'They're charming chaps socially, I'm sure,' he added, with a mocking glance at Ernestine, 'but not very good at their job.'

'Fancy anyone ever being stupid enough to think you were queer,' said Cécile to the king, squeezing his knee.

'Your Majesty,' said Picard, in an official voice, 'I should like, on behalf of my department, to express our condolences on the sad demise of your distant cousin.'

'Oh, that's all right,' said the king. 'I'll be able to find another double. I have quite a lot of cousins.'

Bonpain leaned across to Picard. 'I'm worried about what to do with Gibeau's body, which is back in the cellar of the fish market,' he confided. 'His first funeral was paid for out of police funds, but there'll be questions asked if I charge up another one.'

'I'll see what we can do out of my expense account,' said Picard, reassuringly.

Colonel Withers looked along the table at his old friend, the king. 'Why the hell didn't you go to Paris?' he asked.

His Majesty looked at Cécile and stroked her arm. 'I didn't feel like it,' he said.

'You know that Lloyd George and Asquith and Poincaré and a couple of Russian grand dukes are still there, waiting for you.'

'I still don't feel like it. Ask them to come here.'

But Lloyd George and Asquith and Poincaré and the couple of Russian grand dukes didn't feel like it either, which was one of the reasons why the First World War lasted so long.